All hands were still on deck as dawn began to break. It was a glorious sight, black fading to indigo, made less so by the sight of the white sails of our square-rigged pursuer, only a couple of miles off. I understood they "had the weather-gauge" of us, and that the game was up.

*****

In *Return to Treasure Island*, Karl Moeller has done an extraordinary job in creating a book that not only draws lovingly from the original Stevenson classic, but he has added his own nuances that will delight readers already familiar with the tale.

- Paul Cook, Ph.D, Creative Writing instructor, Arizona State University, published sci-fi author, Tempe, AZ

At last a sequel worthy of its precursor! *Return to Treasure Island* captures the essence and full-bodied spirit of Stevenson's timeless classic. Moeller, like Stevenson, has the ability to surround observation and action with beautifully realized atmosphere and detail. This is the perfect sequel for readers seeking the pleasure of adventure.

- Michael O'Brien, Author & Creative Writing Instructor, Tucson, AZ

Every avid reader knows that wistful feeling: the book has come to an end, but you are not quite ready to abandon its compelling characters. You want to know what comes next! Some authors satisfy this yen by going on to write a sequel, or perhaps a series, but, unfortunately, R. L. Stevenson did not. It is a delight that Karl Moeller has finally stepped up to answer this yearning for countless fans of *Treasure Island*. They will not be disappointed.

- Kathy Hill, Editor, former Director of the Chesapeake Schooner Race, Maharashtra, India

No hackneyed pirate plots here.. an authentic voice, very like Stevenson's own, the perfect sequel to the immortal *Treasure Island*.

- Panhandle Professionals Writing Contest, Amarillo, TX

ISBN 978-0-692-40904-6

Published via www.ingramspark.com

To contact the author: karl.moeller@me.com

Map of Treasure Island rumored to have been drawn by
R.L. Stevenson

Back cover author photograph courtesy of Doug Cox

AMB Publishing resides in the hearts of mankind

Book Layout and Cover Art done in Apple's Pages program
  by Karl Moeller

Modern No. 20 font

Return to Treasure Island

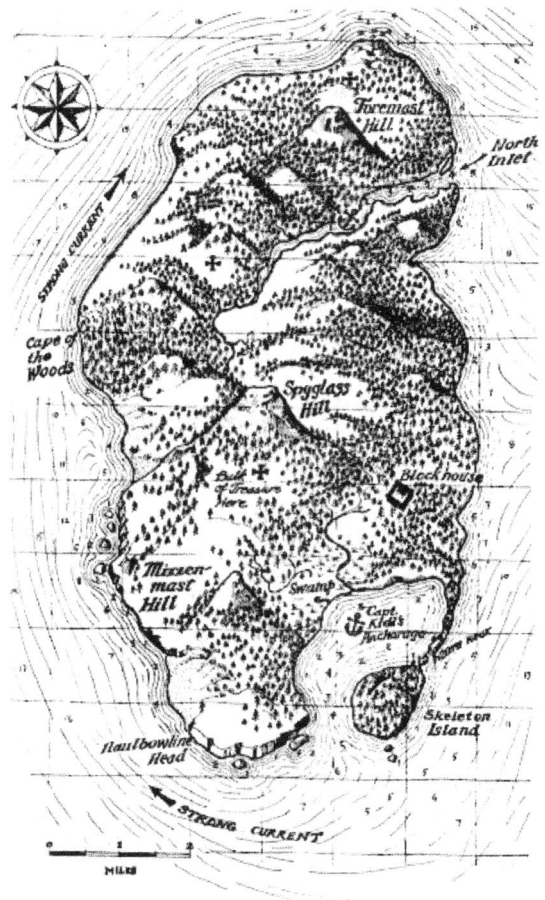

K. E. Moeller

Return to Treasure Island

Call all hands to man the capstan
See the cable run down clear
Heave away and with a will boys
For old England we will steer
And we'll sing in joyful chorus
In the watches of the night
And we'll sight the shores of England
When the grey dawn brings the light

Rolling home, rolling home
Rolling home across the sea
Rolling home to dear old England
Rolling home, dear land to thee

PREFACE
to the current document

Being as the Doctor and the Squire had me write out the original story, and this being the continuation of the story, I had better inform the reader how things lay, as they say. At the conclusion of the previous tale, treasure loaded, our sadly reduced crew headed for England in the Hispaniola. During a stopover for repairs and crew, our sea-cook and betrayer, Mr Long John Silver, who we were transporting to be hanged, escaped from belowdecks along with a small bag of specie. No one registered any regret at his escape; relief was the predominant emotion.

The remainder of our party, Doctor Livesey, Squire Trelawney, Captain Smollett, Ben Gunn and myself, returned home safely. Each used his share of the treasure ill or wisely, according to his nature. Human nature, acted upon by Providence, is at the heart of all good tales. May this one not disappoint.

J. Hawkins.

Return to Treasure Island

Part I. - THIS INSANE ENDEAVOUR

Chapter 1.

The Doctor's Proposal

"Which one are you?" demanded the voice behind the door.

"Uh, Hawkins, Radcliffe Infirmary." It was the agreed-upon hour of the night, and I had knocked using the correct code. Three and then two, or was it two and then three?

"School's out, laddie."

"Not according to Dr Parsons. Open up."

A creature with a lanthorn soon opened the door. "Come in, sor, come in." I hurried after this person, the keeper of the dead, down a stairs and a dark, dank stone passageway. He opened a door and waited for me to enter.

The shifting lamplight showed a row of small, cloth covered forms: this week's crop of pauper children. This was the cellar of the Oxford Town poor-house.

Competition for cadavers had created this appalling necessity.

I asked his back, "Might I take a barrow and do my work at the infirmary?"

"Oh, no, sor, strickly illegal, that is. I have to bury this lot first in morning. I reckon that gives you about six hours o'work right here." He drew back the cover from a grey, pinched little face, eyes staring glassily at the ceiling. "This'n died o' the great pox, she's only aboot ten. Knew her ma. Over here, we have the starvelings, sor. Two on 'em. Just put 'em mostly to rights before you leave, can't have any extra bits fallin' off the waggon, your Honour." He coughed significantly and held out his hand.

I counted out his coppers, and he departed, leaving me in the silence of that cold, dripping cellar room, with only one lantern, in the company of the quietest children imaginable.   Optima philosophia et sapientia est meditatio mortis.   I regretted my choice of vocation extremely at that moment.

I removed my cloak, hung the light as best I could, carefully laid out my drawing paper and pencils, my wiping cloths, my surgeon's kit of scalpels forceps grippers and small saws, and then was sick in the corner. I should have brought a classmate as companion; we could have made our medical-school jokes and turned these poor children into specimens. As bad as this was, dissection was easy compared to actual surgeries. While the patient was rendered as insensible as possible through use of alcohol or tincture of poppy, they still screamed and strained through any surgery: shattering to the nerves, encouraging hasty, often sloppy work.

I did my own grisly work that long, long night, careful to not think about their lives, or look at their faces. That row of little, little bodies, tiny former persons, waiting silently for a coating of quicklime in a pauper's grave, broke my heart. I dutifully took my notes and drew my pictures.

It was raining at dawn when I left the poor-house; hideous pictures filled my head and my portfolio. I walked past the silent cemetery where, at the far edge of the field, a gravedigger prepared a home for my late friends. Averting my head, I turned toward my apartment, where several bottles of good brandy awaited me. My only plan was to get drunk as a lord.

*****

The dead make good neighbours. They never came from their nearby resting places to beat upon my apartment door; they never shouted with Stentorian voice for me to rise from my fog and hearken; they never presumed upon past acquaintance and obligation; they never demanded I wash and dress for an unwelcome excursion. The dead never called me a sodding young pup. Or perhaps it was 'sodden'.

Before the Cemetery of St. Mary of the Virgin had quite faded from sight, Dr Livesey thrust a folio into my hands. "Read this, James," he said, and turned to gaze out the window. Seated in the rattling, jouncing coach, ill in head and stomach, I squinted at the parchments, apparently written with the assistance of a magnifying-glass. It was a chill and rainy forenoon. The horses' iron-shod hooves made an unbearable clatter on the cobbles as we moved briskly south down St. Aldate's Road and across the bridge over the Thames. A brandy would set me right.

Two would be better. I knew several pubs near Templeton College, on our way. However, the grim impatience on Livesey's face told me this would not be well received.

It began "By The Grace of His Majesty King George III, Anno Domini February MDCCLXXVIII." The document was the usual, I suppose, an indecipherable legal snarl of prose intentionally designed to be as opaque in meaning as possible. As an Oxonian, I was literate in Latin (as could be expected), Dominus Illuminatio Mea and all that, but this jumble of legal verbiage only served to inform that one John, Squire Trelawney had been served a writ and condemned at Westminster Assizes, defendant in a suit laid on by a series of organisations with mostly Dutch names.

We had by this time left Oxford Town behind and were now in mostly open countryside, trees still bare, shadowless dim light from grey, leaden skies, traversing a very muddy road, rain drumming on the roof, wheels splashing mud up onto the coach windows. Dr Livesey leaned forward in order not to raise his voice over the carriage. "Trelawney did not merely invest in a losing venture; he was a principal in a Dutch trading company which made rash promises and in his name solicited heavy investment from both Amsterdam and London banks. I fear that his debt is two hundred thousand pounds." I blinked at the enormity of the sum. This, at a time when twenty pounds per year would support a family in comfort; fifty, and you were considered well-off. "Read on, James, read on."

I resumed my squinting for a while, extracting no more new information. Laying the papers aside, I held my aching head in my hands for a moment, then drew my coat closer around me; the damp coach, Livesey's own, smelled like a large wet dog.

Livesey said to me, "The Squire, rightfully apprehending that any opportunity to right these wrongs would be negated should he be unjustly imprisoned, is in hiding from the bailiffs of the court. He requires assistance of us."

I burst out, "'Assistance'! He has contrived to lose more than ten times my net worth!"

"While it is true, James," the Doctor said smoothly, "that there are no laws of man or God that require us to spring to the aid of Squire Trelawney, it is also true that we owe our fortunes to him."

I grumbled, "Much of which I've spent at a school so poorly run I have to pay bribes to dissect."

Livesey paused as the coach lurched through a series of pot-holes. "Without his investment in that voyage 13 years ago, I should not have my estates and you would not have dreamt of Oxford; your mother's inn has prospered and you are quite the figure of a young gentleman."

Irony was not beyond the Doctor. Certain it was I looked no gentleman; I had discharged my man some time before; unable to conceal his opprobrium regarding my habits, he stated he had engaged to be a gentleman's gentleman, with a certain emphasis on the first 'gentleman'; so I had no other recourse than to sack the fellow. Therefore my ensemble still smelt of the grave; it was a squalid, slept-in velvet waistcoat, stained sateen breeches, elegant but mud-encrusted shoes, with unwashed, unpowdered hair, unshaven cheeks, almost exactly like that of a young graduate after a week-long carouse.

I raised my head. "Why do you not sell the Hispaniola and remand the monies directly to the Squire ?" Livesey had bought our old schooner Hispaniola from the Squire some years before, and before the revolt of the American colonies, he had enjoyed several short summer voyages in the Mediterranean, with Captain Smollett presiding. A rich man's hobby.

The Doctor pulled out his pipe and began loading it before replying. "The Squire's debts far outweigh the value of the Hispaniola, being a schooner of only 100 tons, unsuited for heavy trade or war. She is being refitted in a dockyard at Bristol." Apparently realising he had no light for his pipe, he thrust it in his pocket with annoyance. The Doctor had adopted the new gentleman's practice of going without wig, with only a ribbon in his queue, though he was dressed elegantly, as if to a ball.

He looked at me keenly. "You have not enquired regarding our destination. We are going to London and the Savoy."

It was dusk as Livesey's coach picked its way along the Strand toward the Savoy. The rain had stopped and there was a sharp salt breeze coming off the Thames. I looked around curiously; I had been to London before but never to this area. Well built up, but none too prosperous.

Livesey leaned forward. "We are in a foreign dominion, James. The local London and Westminster courts have no jurisdiction here." He paused and looked out the coach window for a moment. "None at all." Seeing my uncomprehending look, he continued, "The Liberty of the

Savoy is the Duchy of Lancaster, where the inhabitants are exempt from the King's writ. The Lancasters, not King George, have sovereign powers in the Savoy."

It was clear, then, why the Squire had gone to ground here. The coach slowed, and we exited, gathering our bags for the walk to the Squire's inn. We stood facing a hive of narrow streets and alleys with crimping houses, pubs, and artisan's workshops. Following Livesey, I plunged in bravely.

As we walked, Livesey told me more about the area; in 1245 Henry III had given the area to the Earl of Savoy, and presently it and its palace descended upon Edmond of Lancaster, and the Lancasters had held the land, and its attendant Liberties, for several hundred years. We passed many a pub named for various Lancasters; Goode Queen Eleanor, John Gaunt's Haunts, et cetera.

"The Squire joins a legion, nay, generations of miscreants eluding the King's Law here in the Savoy," said Livesey, "many of them debtors as well. I believe court bailiffs are enjoined from seizing anyone here excepting those accused of capital crimes. These fugitives may only leave the Liberties each Sunday, being the day of Grace from seizure as well." The people we passed walking (for the streets, alleys, really, were too narrow for most coaches) seemed of every stripe, commoner to Lord. But I had no sense of danger; perhaps in a refuge such as this, petty crime would only serve to attract unwelcome attention. Night was upon us, and I was feeling fairly 'clemmed' with hunger as we arrived at Wood's Inn.

"Welcome!" Squire Trelawney, looking prosperous, threw his door open wide to admit us. As we entered, Trelawney said, "You both know my daughter Lilith."

Lilith was a handsome young woman, nineteen or twenty at the time. A stunning dark brunette with dark blue eyes, she wore a cream-coloured muslin dress of modest cut; tellingly, she wore no jewellery at all. Taking Livesey's hand, murmured, "Doctor." Turning to me, she took my hand, looking in my eyes, said, "Is it 'Doctor' Hawkins yet?" I nodded, still holding her hand, which she gently extricated. She looked me up and down, at my wrinkled reeking clothes, and said sweetly, "How nice of you to include us in your celebratory revels." And she turned to Livesey, whom she had known since childhood.

Over a wonderful meal in his rooms, the Doctor and Squire discussed his case. I was seated across from Miss Lilith and I must say she looked enchanting in candlelight. I ventured, "Miss Trelawney, I am sorry to say the last time we saw one another was not a happy time. I was just back from my little tour of the Continent... that would have been... seventy-four?"

Her face clouded. "No, my mother passed in seventy-three. I stayed as long as Papa needed me. It was very hard." She glanced at the Squire momentarily. "Then I returned to France. It was a second home to me." She brightened, it seemed to me, falsely. "But you are not only a surgeon but an Oxford physician. You must be very excited."

"Oh, yes," I said unenthusiastically. "Excited. I was recalling some of the early days along the coast. I'd see you going past in the Squire's coach.. you looked like a little princess to me then."

"Then you came into your inheritance and went away to school." She turned somber. "Life seems a series of partings at times." And her attention went back to the other end of the table.

The Squire was saying, "...and I heard my creditors were positively foaming because I was beyond their reach, a guest of the Lancasters - though why these chaps would try to toss a fellow in prison, who owed them money, is peculiar. You couldn't begin to pay it back, you see."

His flow of talk was interrupted by a rap at the door, and the Squire admitted a youngish person, perhaps a law-clerk or scrivener, considering his inkstained fingers. This person, dripping water, for it had begun raining again, presented the Squire a message in the form of a letter, declined to stay for a reply, and departed.

Holding the letter to the candelabra, the Squire read aloud:
"John, Squire Trelawney:
My dearest Sir: I am not unacquainted with the merits of your case. My practice brings me in regular intercourse with organisations such as the London and Amsterdam banks that comprise your creditors. I am not so sanguine as to be assured that my reputation precedes me; however, I have discovered certain facts which, presented in the right way, would further your cause and perhaps annul the case against you altogether. As I must leave for the North tomorrow, I propose, Sir, a meeting this very night between Ten and Eleven P.M. I will be at the address below whether you can or no. No reply is necessary.

Your obdt. srvt., Roger North, Barrister, St. John's Wood."

Turning to the Doctor, he said, "He gives directions and his address as well. Livesey, what is your opinion?"

The Doctor frowned. "I have heard the name, though in what context I cannot say. The fellow is certainly acquainted with your circumstances, to dispatch a messenger directly to your door. Though I decry the haste, it is perhaps worth the trip. As it occasions leaving the safety of the Savoy, James and I will accompany you. In any case, it's a filthy night, and our presence abroad will not be remarked." He glanced at me. "We will discuss our plans on the way."

In short order we said our goodbyes to Miss Lilith, donned our cloaks and hats and walked briskly to the Strand side of the neighbourhood, near where Livesey and I had disembarked earlier in the day. It was pitch black and pouring. The occasional street-light made a tiny hole in the gloom. Rather than send for the Doctor's coach we determined to engage one of the many roving hacks along the Strand. One appeared on the port bow, but as the Doctor hailed it, I saw forms moving toward us.

They came out of the gloom, low and fast, sharks after tunny, men in dark cloaks holding cudgels out in front of them, like clasp-knives in a tavern brawl. Livesey, Trelawney and I instinctively got our backs together, facing out; we each had our heavy sticks at the ready. There were four of them, circling fast. Livesey said quietly, "Bailiffs. We must get the Squire back to the Savoy." Calling out to the men circling us, he hissed, "You dolts - it is Sunday and he is exempt!"

"Not yet it ain't, Guv'nor," came from behind me. Strictly speaking, all three of us were breaking the law, by resisting the bailiffs of the court. I did not care. I aimed a killing blow at the one nearest me, but as I moved, he dipped below my arc and almost casually swiped his cudgel across my kneecap and shins, and I dropped in agony, thinking my knee broken. Pain is white, and while I could not see, I could hear a shouted whisper, "Not him, the fat one!" and the wheels and hooves of the approaching coach.

I struggled to a sitting position, seeing Livesey face down in the pouring rain. I looked up to see Trelawney's feet, kicking, as he was dragged backwards, bellowing, into the coach, already moving fast, until it disappeared around a corner.

*****

"Livesey ! Jim ! Thank God you've come !" Squire Trelawney's cosy, quiet tower room had a fire, chairs, bedding, remnants of a meal and brandy on the sideboard, for all the world like his room at the inn. Not too onerous an imprisonment. After all, he was not poor, only in debt two hundred thousand pounds. However, the Squire looked pale and drawn, nearer sixty than fifty, dressed quite plainly, hair loose, hands shaking, whether from drink, illness or emotion, I could not tell. Very changed in a very few days. He grimaced, addressing the Doctor. "That Kapitein was here again, demanding the bearings." The Doctor glanced at him sharply, and the Squire looked away. "Of course I did not tell him, Livesey."

"And well you did not," said Livesey, crisply. "Else we can be certain he will not take us."

While I was puzzling on this, Trelawney had pivoted on his heel and was staring out at the countryside through his single window. This high up, bars were unnecessary. Of course, with less money a gaol could be much less comfortable; the place we were in was reputed to have quite a dungeon. In here, War seemed a distant rumour; in here the American Colonies were still faithful subjects of the King; in here, Britain was not perennially at war with France and Spain. We seated ourselves. I dragged my chair a bit closer to the fire and looked about curiously. The room may have once been painted sort of a yellow; but the paint had mostly worn off, letting the rough-dressed grey granite block show.

"Squire, may I ask, where is Miss Trelawney?" Unaccountably I had hoped to see her, even in a prison.

"This is no place for her," replied the Squire. "she's back in Dorset with my sisters, near your mother's inn on the coast."

The Doctor had at last got his beloved pipe going, and said to the Squire, "My dear, would you tell us how you come to be here? Mr. Roger North, Barrister, professed complete ignorance of this whole affair, and I was compelled to believe him." He patted his pocket. "It is difficult to tell all in a letter."

Trelawney looked around vaguely, as if not really seeing his surroundings. "Ah, yes, that letter. Last I saw you, I was conveyed directly to the Westminster court gaol, easy as kiss my hand."

I felt my left knee; the swelling had gone down, but stairs were still a trial. Livesey looked at me and rolled his eyes slightly; he had his own bruises from that night, and neither of us would term Trelawney's abduction "easy as kiss my hand".

The Squire shook his head ruefully. "I own myself an ass once again, Livesey. That Wollett was there waiting. He is the solicitor for that one Utrecht bank I told you of. He is an insinuating, oily fellow, quite knowledgeable of my affairs, and he kept pressing me, asking did I have access to any funds, anywhere in the world. Pressing hard, I say. Clearly they knew of our treasure voyage, and he intimated that if we were to include the creditors in our plans, that I might be released; thus my letter to you, Livesey." He pleaded, "I had to tell them; I am so very sorry to impose upon our friendship."

The Doctor seemed taken aback and raised his palm to the Squire. "Say no more. I owe you more than I could ever repay. Thanks to you I have lived in luxury, taking Mediterranean voyages in recent summers. Accordingly, the Hispaniola does not need much to be seaworthy. Unfortunately Captain Smollet is steadfast in his retirement, and cannot be budged." There was a lengthy, and, it seemed to me, uncomfortable pause. The Doctor then asked him, "Have any more conditions been imposed, other than this odious Kapitein?"

Shaking his head, the Squire gestured weakly at a large stack of papers on a chest. His voice trembled as he said, "While I was imprisoned in the Savoy, and whilst I rot in here, my family have been evicted from the Manor, and live like farmers in a cottage belonging to a relative. Lilith, the beauty of our family, has been cut dead by society. Contingent upon the success of our voyage, the Manor will be sold by the end of the year. Do you know how long my family has held the Manor? Four hundred years, sir, four hundred years!" He stared blindly at nothing, eyes brimming with unshed tears.

I sat and marvelled. The Squire would dine out on this story for years. The poor fellow, after you got through the bonhomie, had no conversation, never said anything he had not said the day before. He had regaled his fellows with mutineer stories for as long as his fellows would stand for it, or perhaps a bit longer, and of course he told them with never a variation. Society had long since got bored with him, if not his money, all of which led to Miss Lilith not being received. She was a beauty, though, always away at some French finishing-school or another, at least before the War; poor preparation for hard times in a cottage. Restless, I stood. "Gentlemen, it is a cold and rainy afternoon. Some brandy for you?"

Livesey shook his head, lips compressed with annoyance.

"Yes, Jim," mumbled the Squire. He looked around the tower room and continued: "Here things are so convenient, so close at hand, like being on shipboard." Visibly collecting himself, he went on, "Livesey, how do your affairs stand?"

"The Hispaniola will be ready to travel in eight weeks, and so shall I. She is being refitted in one of the smaller shipyards in Bristol. I had to bribe several Admiralty clerks in order to secure sufficient sailcloth and hempen rope to adequately re-rig her. If she were square- rigged the cost would have been prohibitive, but the schooner layout proved affordable."

With half a brandy inside me, I felt much more myself. "Excuse me," I interposed. "So there is a treasure voyage planned in the old schooner. What treasure, pray? And who is this Kapitein you mentioned?"

Trelawney closed his eyes. "My solicitor, that useless baggage..." He paused. "Livesey, you tell it."

The Doctor took a moment before replying. "As you see, Hawkins, the Squire's creditors, a gathering of banks, know of this new voyage. Indeed, it is a condition of his release. Seeing an opportunity, they are imposing some conditions. The primary condition is a sailing captain, ironically named Jos von Loendersloot; a very hard character, as I understand. The crew is not yet chosen." He smiled humourlessly. "As it was quite forcefully explained to me, the alternative to accepting this Von Loendersloot is that the Squire loses everything. Nearly immediately."

"Loses everything? He is here in debtors-prison and his family has been evicted from the Manor! What else is there?"

Trelawney said in a murmur, "They could imprison my immediate family. That is their leverage." His eyes opened, red with rage. "My Lilith in prison - never!"

"As the Squire mentioned," Livesey continued, staring absently into the fire, "the Manor is not yet sold. Should it be auctioned, it would bring tuppence in the pound, and he would still languish here."

"I am most heartily sorry to hear of these events," I said, "but I fail to see why you are informing me with such exactitude. A letter would have sufficed." They exchanged a quick glance.

Livesey spoke gently. "I am fifty. Sound, yet fifty. The Squire is nearly sixty. If this voyage, and the reclamation of the remainder of the treasure, is to succeed, it will be with you, with our common interests, in the vigour of your young manhood, at our sides. While I do not specifically suspect von Loendersloot, I do know that monetary pressure can cause men to bend all law; our past acquaintance with certain 'gentlemen of fortune' well attests to that." He had the grace to clear his throat. "We want you to accompany us as a common man before the mast."

"Return to Treasure Island? Don't you know that it took me years to have a good nights' sleep, to not wake sweating from dreams of blood and killing in that accursed place? I am no sailor -- why do you require my presence on this insane endeavour?" I was on my feet, striding angrily toward the door, a very, very stout door, securely closed and locked against me. I turned back to them, the scheming villains.

Seeing the expression upon my face, Livesey held out a palm. "A moment more, James, please. Trelawney's debt is two hundred thousand pounds. I only know one possible source of that much money. Of course, if you have an alternative suggestion, I should be glad to have it." Receiving no reply, he went on: "None involved in this voyage, including our new captain, knows of your connection with the Squire and myself. If you accept our proposal, you will bunk in the foc'sle and work as a man before the mast. As for your not being a sailor, nonsense. As a boy, with only the help of one badly wounded mate, you sailed our old schooner halfway 'round the island to a safe anchorage. On our voyage home, we were so shorthanded that you worked as hard as any grown man. The war in the American colonies has emptied the docks of common and able-bodied seamen; your presence as a 'green' hand will not be remarked upon. I ask you to hide your education, of which you are justifiably proud, and again be a sailor. Working thus, you will be in an invaluable position to know the temper and intentions of the crew."

"I am certain it would be expedient to have a spy in the foc'sle," I said bitterly. "You recount my experience as if it were an adventure. At age ten, I killed that man !" I paused for breath, still on my feet, fists clenched. I clasped them behind my back. "Doctor, you and I could pauper ourselves to save the Squire from his fate, all because he is a poor investor; instead you ask me to risk my life. Take my money, and let me stay ashore."

The Doctor went on: "I say, the young are always less adventurous than their elders. Please, allow me to finish. All those years ago, whilst we were on the island, I was able to spend some time surveying the remains of Flint's treasure, mostly bar silver, which Ben Gunn had moved and re-buried. Because of this war with the Colonies, the price of silver has more than doubled since our voyage."

"Silver, is it?" I cried. "We'd a bellyful of Silver, and it nearly cost our lives. I shouldn't be surprised but that you had engaged him to be ship's cook, for old times' sake. I said years ago that oxen and wain-ropes would not bring me back again to that accursed island. Quite out of the question, Doctor!"

Trelawney had drained his brandy and was slouched deeply into his chair, completely silent, eyes closed.

"James," said the Doctor, "do you still wish to be a surgeon?"

What an unexpected question -- but, typical of Livesey, completely to the point. He knew me well. Amputations and lancing boils in filthy conditions did not appeal; riding to hounds with a series of delectable companions was more to my taste. "No, sir, I most emphatically do not."

"Can you afford not to work? Can you do anything besides?" said he.

The five hundred I had per year, after sharing with my mother and the family, would not support an estate of much consequence. I had also acquired a taste for baccarat and wagering upon equine velocity. And there was a certain Miss Bellingham, whose elegant manners and porcelain complexion haunted my nights. Trade was unfashionable and its account-books unfathomable. Returning to taverning was unthinkable.

"No," I replied sullenly, "I must earn a living, and I have no other trade."

Livesey then told me, "Then you must trust Providence to show your way." He leaned forward and spoke slowly and forcefully right into my face: "Seven hundred thousand pounds. Without it Trelawney is ruined, as you see. I say to you that if we reclaim the silver, you, I, and the Squire would never want, or have to work, or in his case, invest, again. And unto our descendants also." His eyes gleamed in the firelight. "Though an honest man, I am not without some avarice. I admit in your case adventure is no lure." He looked away. "While youthful revels and drinking-bouts are to be expected at University, you have exceeded even the most liberal standards of behaviour at Oxford; I have it on good authority you graduated by a hairsbreadth -- with much leniency from the teaching staff. This voyage would do you and your character much good. If indeed you can cast a deaf ear to Squire

Trelawney's plight, and you are unmoved at the thought of living as a landed, wealthy gentleman to the end of your days, then I withdraw my proposal and my good countenance."

The wicked, wicked dogs: I was morally certain they had rehearsed this little play, the Squire, injured and weak, playing upon my sympathies, and the Doctor thundering righteously like Jehovah. It was no happenstance that the Doctor had dragged me here this day, locking me in. I stared at him defiantly, and threw myself back into the chair.

Livesey looked up. Even through the thick door we could hear the tramp of boots and metallic jingle of arms; apparently a watch-change.

Trelawney smiled wryly. "A reminder I am decidedly not at home."

A key rattled in the lock and the door opened. A smallish, prosperous looking man in a too-bright cravat walked in, carrying a folio with papers. He was followed by two hulking jailers, one of whom had admitted us earlier.

The Squire stood. "What do you want, Wollett?"

Wollett affected injury. "Not much of a welcome. I'm here wif glad tidings, Squire - you can go free to help to prepare for your voyage, the papers is signed." He looked from the Doctor to me. "Wisitors.. Ain't this nice. Mr. Livesey. " He addressed me. "Mr..?"

Livesey interjected, "Jim."

"I'm right glad you're here, sir," said Wollett. "..the last time we talked I weren't sure the Squire here quite understood the gravity of his situation."

Trelawney sat down again and looked at the floor. He said quietly, "I understood you well enough."

Wollett continued, "Doctor, as the owner of the wessel Hispaniola, you have a certain responsibility." He pulled some papers from a pocket. "For example, neever you nor the Squire seen fit to inform my clients of the bearin's of this alleged island."

Livesey snorted. "And if we give you the bearings, Trelawney here rots in prison, depending entirely upon your 'honour' and honesty. No, the Squire and I are going on this voyage in spite of you and your Dutch Kapitein."

"Fine. You and this old fool go along." Wollett's voice rose and he became red in the face. "Squire, my clients is within their legal rights, in your absence, to imprison any member of your family in your stead - did you know that?"

I know my fists were clenched. The two turnkeys shifted nervously. Trelawney said, bitterly, "Cowards. Cheat me, hold ME responsible --"

Wollett interrupted him. "Your daughter, Squire! If you ain't back, wif the money in.." - he consulted another piece of paper - "..thirty days o'your departure, Miss Lilith Trelawney's comin' here to live." He looked around at the room. "On'y not in these swank digs, oh my no.. she'll be in the basement.. wif the whores and lunatics."

Livesey's voice was tight. "That's inhuman. We can't leave for eight weeks at least. And thirty days - it takes two weeks' sailing simply to get there!"

I had heard enough from this odious little wretch. I grabbed his lapels and jerked him off the floor. "If you touch her you'll answer to me."

One of the jailers moved quickly and pounded me hard in the kidney with his stick. I fell to the floor. Wollett gave me a quick, vicious little kick and then took a moment to straighten his coat and composure.

He said, "And I might take a special, personal interest in her case, gentlemen..   there's costs associated with maintainin' a prisoner here.. I'm sure we could find ways to defray said costs."

Trelawney stood, shaking in anger. "You animal!"

I was back up, ready to lunge at Wollett again. He stepped behind the two jailers, toward the door.   He said, "Two weeks out, two days diggin', an' two weeks back - thirty days. I've got a man watchin' Miss Trelawney, so don't try an' hide her.   Sail quickly, gentlemen.   My clients is impatient men. "   They left the room, leaving the door hanging open behind them.

We all stood in silence for a moment. The Squire cleared his throat. I had never noticed before how grey and thin his hair had become. He stepped over to me and put his hand on my shoulder.   "Jim, I've known you since you were a boy. A fine, brave lad. It is not easy for me to ask you; if not for me, then for Lilith and my family."

I looked longingly at the door, after Wollett the solicitor. "Oh, I'm going."

*****

Several days later, back in Oxford Town, I found myself at the door of a large, prosperous-looking household. The door was opened by the same simpering wretch of a doorman I had encountered previously. This person, resplendent in livery and wig, said, "Mister Hawkins, I regret Miss Bellingham is not at home."

"Not at home? Not at home to me, you mean."

He opened the door just a bit farther and said, in a tone just short of sneering, "Miss Bellingham is... indisposed. However, Mr Bellingham will receive you in the study... Sir."

I was led through a wood-panelled hallway to Bellingham's study. Rising fifty, he used the finest tailors and indeed made a fetish of fashion. He had posed himself carefully, standing next to his ornate desk reading a letter.

Without deigning to look up, he began. "Mr Hawkins. I must own myself taken aback by your precipitate decision to depart upon a treasure-voyage.."

I interrupted, "Sir, a very dear friend of my family is in dire -"

He continued, inexorable, still looking at the letter, "- if in fact this latest story is to be believed. In fact, your purported background is quite suspect -- this tale of how you at ten were a taverners son, at eleven you had ten thousand clear, and a coach and four, strains the hardiest credulity. I had imagined you were a sober, hardworking young gentleman physician-to-be, committed to building a prosperous practice, possibly right here in Oxford Town."

"That's my letter!"

He finally raised his head and looked at me. "Indeed. It is highly unlikely my daughter will 'wait for you' or respond in any fashion whatsoever to these puerile protestations... Hope of treasure, young man, is like the lottery, an entirely unreliable calling. It would hardly do, you running low on funds every few years and running off for yet another voyage." His voice began rising, revealing him to be genuinely angry.   "Indeed, Sir, my considered opinion is that you have obligations elsewhere, and have taken up this absurd story to conceal certain distressing facts.   I have never been enthusiastic regarding any connexion whatever between yourself and my daughter; I consider it, and our acquaintance, at an end. Good day."

Through this prepared little speech, I had exercised all the patience of which I was capable.

"I see. I am a liar, and have concealed bastard children. I have, Sir, called men out for less - but because I would not deprive Miss Bellingham of a father, I take my leave."

I am afraid I banged the front door severely.

*****

If I expected to hear any details of the Squire's financial travails on the coach-ride home to Dorset, I was mistaken. We travelled in a public coach and even on the watering-breaks at inns, Squire Trelawney would only sigh heavily, shake his head, and say, "A bad business, Jim. A bad, bad business." Once he said, "Jim, I worry about Lilith - she's not accustomed to Dorset life, not after France and Paris fashion. I couldn't afford to do anything but get her on the Channel packet home - it still runs though we're at war - but I am afraid she doesn't get along that well with her aunts... no one does."

We made it to Dorset with no mishap, and I left the Squire at a cottage full of Trelawney women-folk - Lilith's aunts being the Squire's widowed sisters. I continued on a few more miles to the Admiral Benbow on the coast and had a reunion with my mother and cousins.

*****

When I approached Trelawney's cottage the next morning, hoping to take Miss Lilith for a ride, there was a two seat chaise or cart lying on its side in the ditch, being righted rather easily by two men. After tethering both my mounts, I gained entry and asked after Trelawney. Lilith Trelawney appeared in the parlour and nodded to me. "Dr Hawkins. Papa is out shooting already, denuding the neighbourhood of game."

After navigating the shoals of Aunts, the Squire's rather elderly sisters, Mrs Bandy and Mrs Bowler, I was introduced to two strangers, a man and wife named Hillbrandt. Mr Hillbrandt, a compact yet powerful looking man, was much at his ease, foot wrapped and elevated, sitting near the fire. His wife had a false, foxy look and sat mute. The story came out that they upset on the lane outside the previous evening after dark, and, Mr Hillbrandt's ankle being sprained, had remained overnight. "On our way toward Lyme Regis," Hillbrandt said, "the day got clean away from us and we were hoping to find an inn before dark."

Mrs Bandy, busy with tea, said, "The Hawkins' inn, the Admiral Benbow, is the nicest inn on the seacoast. Or so they tell me." She sighed. "Not being in funds, we haven't been."

"Oh," said aunt Mrs Bowler, "Mr Hillbrandt, I am told by my niece that Dr Hawkins here is a surgeon and physician. He will attend to your poor ankle."

I bowed and said "Certainly."

Hillbrandt looked alarmed at this statement, and put up a forestalling palm. "Not at all, not at all," he said heartily, "it is doing much better now - in fact I wished to show you ladies how well I do with a cane." He rose and stumped about noisily in the parlour for a moment. "But now I beg to be excused, I am rather weary." And he vanished into the back of the cottage.

Lilith looked at me, and out the window at the two horses eating her aunts' privet hedge, and a smile spread across her face. "Do I gather that you are such a prodigious equestrian, that you ride two horses at one time, standing, Dr Hawkins?"

I smiled in return. "Of course not - I was hoping you would teach me that very trick, Miss Trelawney. Or at least come away riding - down in Lyme today there is a horse-fair, a small circus I understand, and some racing." I paused and turned to the Aunts. "I beg pardon for not mentioning this appointment earlier, but I only heard it last night at the Benbow." To Miss Trelawney I said, "I hoped you were at your leisure... I have heard how much you loathe riding on such a fine day."

She looked warily at her aunts. "It is true my engagement calendar is strangely bare. Aunt Georgina, Aunt Marie?"

Aunt Marie waved a hand dismissively.

Her aunts sounded quite a trial. Riding side by side with me down toward Lyme Regis, Miss Trelawney explained that one of the reasons she stayed away in France so much is that they were always trying to marry her off: "'Sit up straight dear - please attend better to your dress -- perhaps a man should call!' They would parade me around the Manor like a prize sow at auction. But the Manor is gone, and now my value is so diminished they don't even scruple at letting me out unchaperoned."

"Certainly," I said, "there is always family pressure to marry at or above one's own station."

"Like a business transaction, with the value of one's own person being weighed with great exactitude."

"Yes. That is what is so confusing to my dear mother - she is no way certain what my station, or value, might be."

We rode on toward the coast, enjoying the splendid spring day.

I said to her, "By the way, that fellow in the cottage is not injured in the slightest."

"Not injured? Why do you say that?"

I stopped and dismounted, handing her my reins, then looked around and darted off the path for a moment. "This stick is my cane." I removed one shoe. "This pebble is my infirmity. Now I shall walk."

I limped about for a moment, then switched the stick to the other hand. "You see? Your Mr Hillbrandt moves with the stick on the opposite side, which puts more pressure on the supposedly injured limb."

Lilith said, "You have not mistook his right for left?"

I shook the pebble from my shoe and remounted my horse. "No, and the way he twitched away when I offered to examine it was quite peculiar. It is a mystery."

A few minutes later Miss Lilith asked me, "Do you think you shall enjoy the life of a physician and surgeon, Hawkins?"

"I don't know how to answer that, Miss Trelawney. From the outside it appears a noble profession, saving lives; but the reality is that it is poorly paid, generally, and the barber-cum-surgeon onus still lives on. We know appallingly little about the sources of disease and infection; leeching is still seen as a curative, which surpasses all belief. It can be dangerous when dealing with communicable disease, and I know more about the human body's pain during surgeries than I cared to."

She considered this for a moment. "But surely, as an Oxford physician, you could command fees and deal with a higher strata of society?"

"Yes," I said, "an Oxford physician can set up for gentleman in London, and by assiduously and outrageously flattering the fat, hypochondriacal wives of the lesser nobility, a living of a certain sort could be made. But I fear the inner man, my inner man, would die of mortification." A family of quail darted across the road in front of us. "That is why I have some hopes in this treasure-voyage; not only to redeem your family's fortune, but to keep me from abasing myself among minor nobility. It is either that, or disease, amputations and breech-births among the poor."

She rejoined, "I believe you are too quick to discard the very real role of the healer, especially for those unable to normally afford such services. I should despise a man who, in the guise of setting up gentleman, eschewed all honest labour, only rousing himself monthly to journey to his banker's in London. That, too, would cause the inner man to slowly die of mortification."

That didn't sound too bad to me, being wealthy enough to pass the time hunting, riding, reading, travelling, and journeying to my banker's for my interest, though I didn't wish to say so, not wanting to be despised before the act by this lovely young woman. "You may be right. It deserves more consideration."

When we reached the Lyme fair-grounds, set in away from the coast, we dismounted and handed our reins to an ostler, and began our stroll. Hurdy-gurdy music reached us from the far side of the grassy meadow, and we passed a small army of vendors with wonderful-smelling tented booths, trading in hokey pokey, brandy snaps and gingerbread. Lilith seemed to brighten a bit and attend to the day about her.

A large man in a huge hat and striped trowsers came by, sitting atop a tiny waggon, pulled by a matched set of small white mares, all with red ribbons in their manes and tails. He had a megaphone and announced that he regretted to inform that the famed Senor Zanthusi and Miss Arabella would not be appearing, but that in their stead would be Dorset's Own Horton Bros. Dancing Horses, world renowned no doubt.

"Have you ever read or seen Ben Jonson's play Bartholomew Faire?" I asked. She shook her head. I continued, smiling, ".. for if you had you would be on your guard every moment here for cutpurses with absurd names like Moon-calf, Tinderbox-man, Trash, and Nightingale."

Lilith said, "Moon-calf, forsooth. My purse is bare. Hawkins, did you say there were races today? I shrink from freaks and fortune tellers, but I adore horses and racing." She smiled knowingly. "The Squire tells me you are a 'milling cove' of some repute - there are usually pugilistic contests at these fetes."

I said, "I believe I see a banner for the races."

We walked past a rickety helter-skelter, a line of locals rolled up, watching their fellows swing about in undignified attitudes. There was a row of tethered animals waiting to race; they ranged from sleek jumpers hunters and racers to a few ungainly cart-horses, entered by the naive. One especially stood out, a dappled monster four full hands taller than the next smaller horse, improbably attended by a small farm-boy of ten years or so. Its feet were the size of dinner-plates, fringed with hair.

Lilith pointed to it. "I tell you, Hawkins, that beast is descended from La Perche in France, and his ancestors carried Chevaliers in full armour, and being armoured themselves, carried probably a four hundred pound load, on campaigns lasting months.   And to see one run is remarkable - once it gets up to speed, its stride is a third or more longer than these overbred, spindle-shanked hunters and jumpers. - I intend to win some money on that horse." For there were race touts and toffs at every horse-fair, and one could always get a wager down.

"Hope springs eternal, Miss Trelawney."   It looked a plodding ox to me; I had my eye on a slender bay at the end of the row, one with a rider and rig far more sophisticated than the rest of the entries.

"Let's go meet the horse and young rider, if indeed he is," said Lilith, and we crossed over to them.   She said, "Good day, young master, we would like to meet you and your horse."

He looked up at her adoringly.   "I'm Jeremy, Miss. And this is Boukephalos, after King Alexander's horse. He's a Percheron.   They carried knights-errant. It means 'Ox-head'."

"Yes, I know."   She smiled and patted the mountain of muscle, indeed as big as an ox, and he snorted and stamped.   "I am Miss Lilith, Master Jeremy, and this is Doctor Hawkins."   Jeremy made his leg to her, ignoring me. She continued, "And does Boukephalos like to run?"

He brightened and piped, "Oh, yes, Miss, he always did. Our land is next a huge moor, and since he was a foal he loved to get loose and run there. At first we chased him, Miss, but he always come back, and we soon learnt to let him loose, like a dog."   He looked doubtfully at me, and back at Lilith.   "You're the prettiest girl I ever did see, Miss - if you was sellin' kisses I'd give all I had!"

Cheeky little devil. She dimpled. "Are you his rider, Master Jeremy?"

"Yes, Miss. When he was a yearling, Dad let me start riding him bareback, and we run for hours across the moors, up and down the coast. Fast as wind, he is, arter he reaches his gallop." He smile shyly. "I can barely hold on."

Lilith turned to me. "There you have it. Lightly laden, he cannot lose. Lend me five pounds and I'll turn it into a hundred." She shook Jeremy's hand and wished him luck in the race. Two steps away, she turned and rushed back to Jeremy, kissing him soundly, saying, "You and Boukephalos win for me."

A few minutes later we found a loudly-dressed fellow who introduced himself as "Trusty Edgeworth - nevver slid out in the midst of a race like some I might mention - (here he nodded his head at a similarly dressed fellow on the far side of the clearing, near the horse-auction) and, unlike some I might mention, I gives fair odds."

I asked, "How long is the race?"

"Five miles, three times round that meadow, sir."

Lilith handed over her borrowed fiver. "On the big Percheron, please."

Edgeworth did not quite snort, wrote down the sum and while handing her a ticket, said, "That fine animal is on for twenty to one odds, Miss. And you, sir?"

"Ten on the bay at the end."

He shook his head. "You mean Mr Barry ridin' the Earl of Lancaster, that's wot they named him. Sorry, Sir, odds is even on him. I can't pay out if he wins - because he always does." He looked fondly at Lilith. "It's sportin' types like this young lady that makes racin' such an absorbin' and lucrative pastime."

"Very well," I said to Lilith, "I shall not bet and shall instead root for that monster of yours - though I expect to see it pulling a haywaggon tomorrow."

She laughed, her first that day, and slipped her arm through mine. "On a sprint or short course I agree with you, Doctor. But over five miles these slender overbred spindleshanked ponces will show their lack of bottom - I'll bet on the rustic over the sophisticate every time."

A crowd of several hundred spread along one side of the impromptu grass racetrack, farmers, local gentry, and sleek imports from places more fashionable. There were about twenty horses entered, spread across the starting line, a rope held by two men on either side of the track. My favourite, the bay, pranced excitedly, the tiny Mr Barry holding him back with great difficulty. The horn sounded, the rope dropped, and they were off; Lilith alternated jumping and waving wildly with grasping my upper arm with bruising strength. I didn't mind a bit.

She proved a better judge of horses than I. After a dismal, lumbering, slow start, her choice's longer stride ate up the course. Young Jeremy must have gotten a mass of bruises from being bounced around on his giant steed. Closing the distance to the leaders, the dappled Percheron's superior stamina, gained no doubt from dragging heavy waggons up-hill, proved too much for the 'over-bred, effete' competition. In short, Boukephalos and Master Jeremy won Lilith her hundred pound. Earl of Lancaster placed second, five lengths or so back.

The fellow with the megaphone rode by on his waggon again, repeating the message that trick riding, comic feats and ropedancing on horseback with the famous Horton's Dancing Horses could be seen in ten minutes in the big tent, and that the great Zanthusi and Arabella were still indisposed.

Lilith triumphantly returned my borrowed five, presented an astounded Jeremy with twenty pounds, and pocketed the balance. "That ought to settle my aunts' hash - no money for dresses, forsooth."

During our late afternoon return from Lyme Regis, trotting along, I was trying to 'post' on my horse to lessen the impact on my gluteus maximus and medius, when Lilith said to me, "On the ride out, you mentioned the treasure-voyage. I fear for my father - he married late in life as you know... he is sixty." She thought for a moment. "Being suddenly poor is so galling to him, and so he will go off to sea again. And I worry. But sometimes I think that staying and being poor would kill him as surely as the sea. Prison is not a healthy place."

"Are you asking me about our odds for success?"

"Yes."

"Candidly, Miss Trelawney, I do not know. It is true that a great deal of bar-silver was left when we departed that island all those years ago, and Livesey tells us that silver is worth far more now, because of this war. So the means are there, at least conjecturally, to bring your way of life more in accord with your experience. But it is war-time, and every sail will be a hazard."

She rode silently.

After some consideration, I said, looking straight ahead, not at her, "There is a matter of some delicacy. The Squire believes you should not be alarmed. I believe you made of sterner stuff. Though I go against the Squire's fatherly request, I must tell you -- tell you that the creditors, in order to ensure our utmost efforts to return, have issued a threat against you personally."

Lilith turned in her saddle and stopped her horse, dark blue eyes upon me. "Tell me."

I reined in as well. Wishing I hadn't broached the subject, I said, "The creditors, in the form of this odious little solicitor Wollett, have imposed a very short time for our return - allowing only thirty days there and back."

"That's absurd!"

"Of course it is. That's not the worst of it. If we don't return within thirty days, this Wollett claims to have the legal right to clap any member of the Squire's immediate family into debtor's prison. You were specifically mentioned. And the quarters are likely to be quite unpleasant."

She considered this, head tilted slightly, as our horses moved and stamped a bit. "Though I wish myself safely away in France, it is no refuge now." She looked right into my eyes. Such an incredible blue. "If I am taken to prison, I shall endure it as bravely as I know how."

"I know you will." I felt a vast pressure of emotion in my chest, a desire to protect her. This would never do.

In a tremulous voice, she said, "Thank you for telling me, Hawkins.   I would rather know than be surprised at midnight by some bailiffs at the door."

"We shall do our utmost to return on schedule," I concluded lamely, and clucked to my horse.

We rode silently for a few minutes, and passed next to the local stables where I saw Hillbrandt's cart inside the barn; off to the side was a small enclosed paddock with several horses. A mare and her week-old foal were ambling about. I had had a noseful of horses for the day, but Lilith said, "Oh, how dear."   We rode over, dismounted, and entered the paddock, carefully avoiding various equine accidents. The foal came to her fearlessly and Lilith said, gently petting its slender neck, not looking at me, "I'm so glad they don't take the mothers away when they're too young."

One of the horses present was a short white mare grazing. Lilith touched my arm.   "Oh, look, Hawkins - the Hillbrandt's cart-horse. I want to see how she's doing." She approached Hillbrandt's horse, which stopped eating and watched us with a placid eye.   It had pert, red ribbons entwined in its mane and tail.   Lilith moved expertly around it, examining for injury, finding none.   She straightened and said "She's fine, aren't you, old girl?" And she slapped the horse's neck as some will do, horses being so large. Suddenly the horse crumpled on its side, eyes wide open. "Oh, dear, can't you get up?" cried Lilith. Almost in answer, the horse gathered its limbs and stood up gracefully.

"What was that about? I said. "She fell when you slapped her here." The spot did not seem bruised or swollen.

The horse performed its trick twice more, getting up on cue. "This horse has been trained to fall," she said. "How strange."

We retreated to our horses and remounted. Before we started up, I said, "Pray tell me everything that happened last night regarding the Hillbrandts."

She paused for thought. "Mrs Hillbrandt came to our door well after dark, about nine o'clock, and entreated us to bring a lanthorn. The cart was on its side, as you saw, and so was this horse, lying patiently in its traces. I followed when the Squire and his man carried Mr Hillbrandt inside. I assume someone released the horse and put it in the paddock last night."

I said, "I have nothing to offer except to repeat two observations: that Mr Hillbrandt shrunk away when I offered to examine him, and that his performance with the cane was ludicrous. No, three - consider the decor in this horse's mane and tail."

"I believe we are being practised upon," she said. "I could even believe that crash was staged in some fashion. In any case that man is perfectly well enough to travel, and they are not staying another night under our roof."

In short order we had Hillbrandt's horse and cart brought round, and Lilith drove it while I followed on horseback. Lilith stormed into the cottage, and over the aunts' and the Squire's confused protestations about hospitality and guests, fairly evicted the Hillbrandts. A guest is not always a jewel resting on the cushion of hospitality. Mr Hillbrandt 'limped' resentfully toward the horse-cart.

"Mr Hillbrandt." I pointed at his foot. "This morning it was the other leg that was lame."

He glared at me with hatred, stumbled as if to modify his gait, and gave it up. His wife helped him up into the cart, slowly, playing for time and to the sympathies of the shocked aunties and the Squire Trelawney.

Lilith walked to the white mare and held her hand up as if to slap it on its neck. With a glint in her eye, she said, "This horse has an unexpected little trick - shall I show you?" The look on the couple's faces was priceless. Lilith stepped back and called, "Mr Zanthusi!" The Great Zanthusi and Miss Arabella looked shocked. Lilith then said, "We missed you at the Lyme horse-fair today, but were able, all the same, to have seen your little act." She was magnificent. A red-faced Zanthusi shook the reins and the cart pulled away up the road.

Lilith turned to the Squire and the aunts and said, "Have any of you seen anything missing or amiss in the cottage?"

Trelawney said, "Well, yes, my dear, this morning I noticed someone had rummaged about in my writing-desk, and assumed one of you were searching for something."

Both the sisters denied any such action; after a few moments' talk they and the Squire turned around and trudged back up the path to the cottage, leaving us standing by the road.

Lilith said to me, "Doctor Hawkins, we are mightily obliged to you for your part in revealing this couple as miscreants under our roof."

I bowed grandly. "My pleasure, Miss Trelawney."

She met my eyes directly, searchingly. Such a look. "And thank you for the outing."

I cleared my throat. "Miss Trelawney, this is entirely premature and inappropriate. We barely know each other as adults - but somehow, this day, without my willing it, you have become dear to me."

She nodded slightly as if she'd known it all along, eyes searching mine, and placed her palm momentarily on my left shoulder. "Come back again, Hawkins."

Schooner

Hispaniola

Chapter 2.

Berthed In Bristol

Eight weeks later I was in a coach rattling toward Bristol Harbour and the old Hispaniola.   Nothing was agreed upon but it was clear to me I cared for Lilith a great deal. Her character, looks, and intelligence recommended her; her family's financial woes had temporarily placed us on a level; indeed, between the Admiral Benbow and my income, I was as well off as the Trelawneys. But would a young woman, educated in France, wealthy again, wish to be wife to a taverner's son, however nouveau riche, however barely-graduated Oxford physician?   I knew she enjoyed my company, but her circumstances in Dorset, beset by two Aunts, were not the best, and I may have been merely a means to escape.   Everything was in mid-air until our return from the voyage, if indeed we did return.

I reflected upon the previous voyage, thirteen years before. The downfall of the voyage stemmed from the Squire's hasty and intemperate choice of crew, trusting wholly in the hearty nature of Silver, while dismissing Captain

Smollet's very strong objections.   The Squire's idiocy in hiring 'salty men before the mast' had brought us a crew of wicked, lawless cutthroats indeed; men who had sailed, not with Hawke, but with Flint -- this new adventure would take me from Oxford back to a world where the only law was force of arms.

I turned over my hands, looking at my scarred knuckles with a faint smile of recollection. Upon completion of my primary education, it was the collective wisdom of the pseudo-genteel set to which my little money had allowed me entry that a 'continental education' would be just the thing. With economy in mind, I embarked upon the usual young gentleman's round of France, Italy and the Germanic Kingdoms. I found French gentlemen, while no doubt deadly with a sword, to be so effete in converse and feminine in appearance as to not excite any emulation in my person; and while the towns and women of Italy were charming, and I learned to tinkle   a bit in the counterpoint upon virginal and harpsichord, and to recollect my Tintoretto from my Titian, overall I found Italy too slight to engage my attention for long. Germany, to my surprise, was more to my taste; I must own that I enjoyed the rounds of following the Jaegermeister after harts, more copious drinking, occasional study at Heidelberg, and learning to duel -- after all, I'd already killed my man.

Thus, with hands hard from rein and sword, upon my return to England and admission to Oxford, I found myself drawn to the practice of scientific pugilism, and joined the Millers, a club of like-minded young gentlemen from the University. Some coves had begun calling it 'boxing', though the only gifts imparted were contusions. From time to time our group would meet a challenge from clubs elsewhere, and I gained quite a good record, against some opponents quite out of my weight.

I also studied fencing in earnest, although I now doubted the efficacy of a foil or epee' against a crude buccaneer's sabre wielded with bad intent. These fighting skills I developed paid handsomely when we got in scrapes between 'town and gown' at some of the low Oxford dives we were wont to frequent. Of course, in the past year, the drinking had quite overcome the fencing and pugilism, and I had not raised a hand in exercise.

Outside the window slowly-greening rural England slowly jolted by, backward. Planting was under way everywhere.

Why was I going to Bristol and join this wretched voyage? I had fought this battle time and again in my mind the past weeks. In one sense I had much to gain. Our course of study now over, my classmates were scattering around the British Isles. Some, like myself, were to begin the tiresome and often repugnant duties of the practising physician. Other classmates had left Oxford to the leisure of a gentleman's life. The aristocracy, beneficiaries of the gulf between the favoured and the merely fortunate, are as enamoured of bloodlines as a breeder of Corgies. However, financial pressures were slowly eroding this monument to pedigree. The gentleman student, likely as not to be deeply in debt to the haberdasher's, I had seen time and again, was rarely averse to scupping a fiver from the better - heeled.

Mulling purchased peerages, I recalled a former classmate, one Welsby, long since gone from Oxford, a repulsive toad, a cringing, fawning creature whose false obsequiousness had nearly earned him a thrashing; Welsby's father, a lowly trader in iron, suddenly and inexplicably became rich as Croesus, through inheritance or crime, and after some legal fol-de-rol must needs be addressed as 'Mossway, Earl of Croxteth'. This selfsame spot-faced homunculus son of an Earl had recently married a glorious piece I once sighed upon from afar, the luminous daughter of Lord Skelmersdale, who was now rumoured to be delivered from heavy debt.

Seventy miles is a long day, in a coach. In the jouncing Bristol coach, my companions, though dressed well enough, could have stood a decent bath. One of them, a demented-looking parson in a broad brimmed black hat, muttered Scripture continuously under his breath, apparently finding some refuge in the Lord. I cut the chill with a tot from my brandy-flask, found refuge in a scented handkerchief, and then reread a recent letter from Dr Livesey.

Dr James Hawkins
Broad's Inn, St. Aldate's Rd., Willamsley, Oxford
April Anno Domini 1778
My Dear Hawkins:
Re yrs. Sunday ultimo:
I am quite in agreement with your views. This Voyage is quite hazardous. First, we are headed for the Caribbean, the last Haunt of Pirate Crews like Flint's, Kidd's, Blackbeard's et cetera, considered long dead or gone to ground. Secondly, because of the Hostilities, declared and undeclared, between England, our American Colonies, France, and, to a lesser extent, Spain. These Powers are struggling for Control of the High Seas. American and French Privateers and Ships-of-the-Line will be the true Hazard upon this Voyage, attempting to commandeer or sink any Vessel flying the Union Jack. Spanish Men-of-War are allied with the

Rebels. The Voyage out will be hard enough; the Voyage back, with the Treasure actually in the Hold of the old Hispaniola, will be a thousand times more hazardous; if boarded, we are certain to be discovered, our Cargo seized, and the Crew possibly impressed.

yr obdt srvt

Livesey

Post Script -- Mind the Press in Bristol

I folded the letter and sat back, smarting resentfully. There was little else discussed in the student pubs at Oxford; according to what I had already heard at University and read in the London press, the rebellion in the American Colonies, now in its third year, and the recently signed treaty between the Colonies and France, made seamen, common and able, scarce on the docks of most seaports. Spain and Holland were rumoured to be considering throwing in with the American Colonies as well. The monetary lure of the prize business created ship's consortiums, legalised piracy, called privateers; their captains and mates, no fools, chose the most qualified, (or at least not habitually drunken) seamen available on the docks. Those still ashore must be dregs, indeed. Thus I decided to take stock of the scuttlebutt about the docks, and make enquiries in the taverns near where the Hispaniola was docked. This would arm me with knowledge of the quality of men presenting themselves as crew members.

*****

The experience of wandering the Bristol docks was peculiar. I knew the town fairly well from having walked it so much as a boy; but much of the walking had been with Long John, and my feelings about him were still atangle after all these years. A blackguard and a murderer many times over, and still at times I missed him. The same grizzled, villainous types still loitered in dockside taverns, swilling rum and telling lies about their service. Thieves of both sexes walked the streets, eyeing anyone with the look of silver about him. I carried my heavy silver-headed stick and when required I slapped it meaningfully in my gloved palm, and accordingly I was left alone. It was late April, and the days were still cool. Here and there a few Negroes in livery walked purposefully on errands for their owners. This was wartime, and labourers with stores bustled them down every thoroughfare to dockside. Horses clattered down narrow cobblestone streets, pulling iron-shod waggons with goods of every kind. The occasional Royal Navy officer in dark blue coat and stand-up collar strode self-importantly on mysterious errands. I walked along with my kerchief to my nose, not relishing the docks' usual piscatory fetor - they stank of untold generations of dead and rotting fish.

The sun was getting high as I took a turn along the Quay, or Key, as the inhabitants call it. This was where the ship traders lived, usually right above their warehouses anent the docks. Because of the war, there were more ships alongside than normal, due, I supposed, to lack of hands and riskier conditions. A veritable forest of spars and rigging, through which one might on occasion espy some grey skies. Bristol has an astonishing tide, almost thirty feet, twice a day; this was high tide, so the decks were on a level with the wharves. Walking along, champing a roll bought from a street-vendor, I tried to fashion a humorous anecdote with which to torment Livesey, an admirer of the plays of Wm. Shakespeare, but it would not come; it featured a pub and two extremely impatient fellows named Tom and Tod.

On the side of a warehouse building, with the remnants of thousands of like flyers fluttering in the breeze, I encountered a recruitment poster for our voyage - bold print, with a black border of entwined cable:

HEARKEN ALL SEAMEN, or STOUT HANDS

Captain Jos von Loendersloot
And the good 100-tonne Schooner

HISPANIOLA

Will embark upon
A Warm Weather Voyage of TRADE
TEN to TWENTY WEEKS in Duration

To various Ports of Call in the
Caribbean.

Top wages and working conditions in
a fast, newly-REFITTED Schooner.

Able-bodied Seamen, Ordinary Seamen,
Landmen, Carpenter and Boatswain are
INVITED to enter on board

HISPANIOLA

Docked at Huffing's Warehouse, Quayside, Bristol

FRIDAY, MAY the First,
Anno Domini 1778.

Walking on, I came abreast of a long low three-mast frigate-looking ship, and had the misfortune for the wind to shift. The smell made the docks seem positively appetising. Her stern bore the appellation 'TEYE BA', and in smaller letters beneath, Whydah. Though the ship seemed deserted, the lines and the stench bore mute testimony as to its purpose. This was one of the famous 'blackbirders' that collected slaves in the African port of Ouidah. Carrying trade goods from Bristol, the ship would land in West Africa, offloading cargo and taking on from 500 to 700 slaves; four weeks later, if the weather was favourable, the blacks still living were traded in the Caribbean for New World gold, silver, sugar, indigo, and for the physician's source of quinine, chinchona, all of which came back to England.

Oddly, considering her purpose, the lines of the ship were beautiful; depending on speed in stead of armament, there was a very short slave deck where a frigate would have a gun-deck. Only four to five feet tall, the deck contained irons for hundreds of humans, who were locked flat to the deck during the month or longer voyage to their new imprisonment. I and all my fellow Oxonians, at least the students, were ardent Abolitionists. The trade had long since lost any semblance of respectability, save among those for whom capital increase is all. In many quarters, holding slaves was considered quite unseemly and even coarse. I realised how few black faces one really sees in Britain. Were they happier away from Africay? Certainly I was modern enough to not ascribe instant happiness as a concomitant of conversion to Christianity; every county had its allotment of miserable, pecksniff parsons.

The Hispaniola, which had been in the dockyards for some time, was now nearly ready to sail. She certainly looked smart enough to me.   My observations were of a covert nature, out the window of a dockside tavern where I settled with some brandy.   The shop had a weathered sign over the door, 'Pig And Whistle'. I smiled when I saw it. Sure enough, while filling a piggin with ale, the barmaid whistled all the while to demonstrate that its contents hadn't migrated to her insides.   After sitting a while, watching life in the Harbour, I asked the owner what he knew of "that little ship over there".

He replied, "Aye, young sir, she's for treasure, that's sure. Caribbean treasure, I hear. Every Man Jack o' Chips (ship's carpenters) that's been workin' her these weeks knows."   It had to be Trelawney, dining out on his new stories all over Bristol, depriving a village somewhere of an idiot.   The taverner paused to pour a tumbler of rum for a customer, a man with the look of the sea about him. It would be rum, every ship's dog drank rum. I never liked it.   He resumed: "And every wharf-rat and cutpurse in Bristol knows."

As I paid my score I admitted I might soon be aboard.

The tavern owner said, "Your ship, eh?" He rubbed his stubbled chin, looked right, then left. 'Tell your Cap'n beware. The crew he gets mayn't be the crew he wants."

Walking along, I had been inadvertently following a family at some distance -- three small towheaded boys, their bonneted mother, and the father, Jack ashore, burly and moustachioed, with the sailor's rolling gait, as if he were still leaning against the ever-moving sea.   Round the corner came a group of men, crossing the street directly toward us. There were two scarlet-coated Royal Marines with muskets and fixed bayonets, a Royal Navy officer, and   five seamen wearing long baggy trousers, brown jackets and round hats. Two of the seamen grasped the father's arms. A Marine shouted, "Press Gang, in the King's Name!" The father, apprehending the situation, began struggling and roaring out that he had a Protection, somewhere, if they would only stay a moment. The mother fluttered around the periphery of the group, screaming incoherently, and the boys stood stock still, in shock, the smallest weeping silently. The officer withdrew a warrant from his bosom, and began reading from it in a low voice, as if his wild-eyed victim were listening, "In the Name of our glorious King George III and the Admiralty..."

I rushed forward toward the group, calling, "One moment, Lieutenant!" as loudly as I could, in that upperclass fluting tone I knew so well how to affect. The officer stopped his reading. By this time I had elbowed my way through the crowd to the side of the impressed sailor, imperiously gesturing his captors aside. I touched his shoulder and back solicitously.

Addressing the Lieutenant, "I, Sir, am a Physician and Surgeon. This man" - and I dug my thumb as hard as I could into the sciatic nerve in his lower back, which runs down into the leg - "is no more than a cripple. I was observing his gait even as you accosted him, Lieutenant, and this man has been shot through the hip at one point." Turning to the father, I said, "What is your name, my good man?" And I pressed even harder on the nerve.

He was in pain, but mumbled, "Durling, your Honour."

I continued, "You were doubtless injured in the service of our King, poor fellow. Durling, would you walk for us?"

The Lieutenant had found his voice. "Now see here, you are interfering in the King's business... Sir."

I leaned toward the officer, still pressing on Durling's back, and said softly, "Ah, Lieutenant, how happy would your Captain be, bringing in a cripple only good for hauling on a line? Let the fellow show us how he walks."

The young officer nodded reluctantly, and the sailors stepped back from Durling, whom I instantly released. He took one step and almost fell, and tried to walk, listing severely to one side, as if game in the hips for years.

"Durling, come back now," I called. He returned, wincing with each step.

I turned to the Lieutenant. "As I say, Sir, you are well rid of this one; neither your Doctor nor your Captain would thank you, hauling in the likes of him."

The officer, a smooth-faced youngster, had begun stuffing the impressment papers in his busom even before Durling turned back toward us. He looked at Durling and said, "Off with you - you're exempted." With that the press gang marched smartly down the block and around the corner, leaving me with the grateful Durling and his family.

After I extricated myself from their clutches, I resumed my walk, considering how differently it might have ended, watching the press gang retreat the way they had come, dragging their prey with them, until they disappeared around the corner, followed by the distraught wife and her three fatherless boys. I mused on the difference, if any, between the status of a Negro slave, and that of a fellow British citizen, dragged off the street and imprisoned on a vessel in the Royal Navy, to work, life continually in danger, or to be flogged to death. I believe I was low in spirits.

*****

"It was remarkable to hear Entwistle's story," remarked Dr Livesey, seated in Trelawney's spacious room in Bristol's Old Anchor Inn, puffing on his everpresent pipe, "...most unexpected at a meeting of the Royal Society. Entwistle and his companions were returning to England from New Spain and the Caribbean on a fast trader when the ship was intercepted and hailed by a heavily-armed cutter flying the Union Jack. They said they'd been out patrolling two months and wondered if the trader would take aboard some mail, and if they had any fresh provisions. As the cutter hove to, fortunately one of the trader's mates recognised the ship for a rebel, and they threw on sail, caught a breeze and were out of cannon range in minutes, with little damage. Those officers were wearing uniforms almost identical to those of the Royal Navy. Apparently they were prepared to board and seize the trader. Later the mate told them the cutter belonged to the rebel captain Gustavus Coyningham, who has a reputation as a privateer. Quite an adventure for a scientist."

"I wager it made you long for the open seas again, Livesey," cried the Squire, clapping the Doctor on the shoulder. Though he affected a hearty countenance, Squire Trelawney was not the man he had been. He had been quite busy since his release from debtors-prison; mostly eating, apparently. Like a huge lobster in brocade, his face was flushed, he was again quite overweight, and his hands were still palsied. His wig was well-powdered, and the plummy peer-of-the-realm accent was in place again.

The Doctor had seated himself in a wingback chair near a window overlooking Bristol Harbour and the River Avon. "Hardly. The fellow's tale was quite hair-raising.' He glanced around. 'And quite an example of what awaits us. No incompetent, drunken pirates this time."

Trelawney frowned and gestured broadly with his brandy glass. "Nonsense. The Hispaniola is a stout ship and has been re-rigged. She now carries more sail than a schooner has a right to, and with her shallow draft and clean bottom, ought to be able to outrun anything on the high seas." He settled back in his chair. He fancied himself quite a sailor, did the Squire.

I turned to the Doctor. "Where we are headed, Caribbean waters, are the last place in the Atlantic to be infested with pirates. Speed does no good if one has already been boarded."

Dr Livesey replied, "I am concerned about the calendar. We must depart within the next two weeks if we are not to brave winter weather upon our return. I should not fancy going aloft in a gale with the temperature below freezing, with ice upon the decks."

I reflected that Dr Livesey's presence up in the yards was extremely unlikely. Unfortunately the same was not true for me. I had taken a small room some distance from the docks and secured clothing appropriate to my newly assumed station: a stylish ensemble of slightly-tattered sailcloth and rough shoes. Listening with half an ear to the conversation, I spied a brandy-flask and began edging toward it.

According to the Squire, Kapitein von Loendersloot was bringing or had brought part of a crew from Amsterdam, men he had sailed with in the past. Of course the thought in all our minds was the loyalty of those men, which would be to their captain, not the ship nor the ship's owners. The Doctor had taken care to conceal the fact he spoke some Dutch. He said, "Some might consider a Dutchman to be a Butterbox, or a stupid German with marbles in his mouth; but the Dutch have been indefatigable sailors, traders and colonisers for two hundred years. Their banks, as we have seen, dominate Europe's economies. Do not underestimate them or their captain."

I interrupted his thoughts by asking a question that had been in my mind for some time. "Doctor, Flint's map which led us to the island had the bearings written on it." Livesey nodded in assent. "And that you delivered the map into Silver's hands. Silver had the map in his possession until the rout at the treasure's original burial site." He again nodded to me. "If Silver had had the map overnight," I reasoned aloud, "He would know the location of the island. What has led both you and the Squire to think that the island has not been plundered by Silver sometime in the past thirteen years? One assumes there are pirate navigators, able to handle chronometers, compass, and sextant."

Toward the end of this speech of mine, Livesey began smiling wryly. "Ah, you must not have noticed that the map, always a ragged parchment, was missing the corner where Flint or Billy Bones had written the bearings of the island. I had torn it off and dirtied it to match the night before I handed it over." He paused a moment, flicking some imaginary dirt off his shoes. "Hawkins, we have not enquired regarding your journey."

I certainly felt that second brandy burning in my stomach. "The journey was uneventful, the usual broken wheels and mud-bogs. The problem is what I discovered upon my arrival here in Bristol."

They exchanged a glance. The Squire leaned forward. "And what might that be, lad?"

"It might be that every rum-pot in Harbour knows that we've a treasure-voyage going," I said, harshly. Trelawney looked stricken. I went on, "Every cut-throat character in every pub up and down the Avon must know. It certainly did not come from me. Doctor, have you any idea how this might have got about?"

The Doctor's face had closed remarkably. Without a glance at the Squire he said, "No. However, it does not signify; we still have a hire-date and a departure-date. It is unfortunate, and I agree we might collect some dockside vermin as a result; we were all aware of that possibility in any case."

Squire Trelawney had turned about in his seat to where he was side-on to us both; he did not seem eager to look us full in the face. I was not inclined to mercy. "Squire, may I enquire how long you have been here in Bristol?"

Still staring off, Trelawney got very red in the cheeks, and blustered, "Hang it all, a fellow can't be expected to watch every little word when he's just got out of gaol, dealing with the relations, securing apartments, packing for a voyage, chivvying the dockyard, entertaining, quarrelling with the printer, and dealing with that blackguard the Kapitein." The Squire was indignant about the Kapitein. "By Jove, he stood before us, proud as you please, and announced in that accent that our cargo would be rotten hides. Perfect for fertilizer, obtainable at any port, and perfect for discouraging inquiries as to what lies beneath."

Privately, I agreed with the Kapitein. Green hides would effectively conceal our true purpose, though I dreaded living with the stink. "Then he went on to tell us, the dog," cried the Squire, "that the Hispaniola was 'too pretty' and that the new paint was to be dirtied, because if we were to purport to carry hides the ship must look the part. Dirty. Philistine!"

Schooner

Hispaniola

Chapter 3

Aboard The Hispaniola

The actual selection of the remainder of the crew went very quickly. It took place aboard ship, with the would-be mariners escorted one at a time into the captain's cabin. The crowd waiting to be interviewed was a diverse one; there were a smattering of landsmen like myself, farm boys looking for adventure, or a berth. The seamen appeared, almost to a man, tattooed, dissipated, destitute, and overfond of drink. Since Captain Cook's famous voyage some years before, it seemed every sailor was bent on decorating as much of his epidermis as possible.

As I awaited my turn, I looked around the Hispaniola curiously; it was all very much smaller than I remembered. Though there were more spars and rigging than I recalled, I could still see the crosstrees far above where, freshly stabbed, I had shuddered and fired two pistol rounds directly in Israel Hand's face. And the deck there where I had sat bleeding, nearly insensible, while an empty bottle rattled around in the scuppers like a frenzied little animal. No, the old ship, refitted and clean, had few charms left for me; and I wondered how the crew's quarters in the foc'sle had been fitted. Dark, I reckoned, fishy and smelling of tar.

The coxswain, resplendent in a black coat and tricorner hat (which I never saw him in again), would appear periodically and bawl, "Volgende!" for the next man. In this way my education in Dutch began. A small crew, perhaps the Kapitein's imports, apparently chartered to slop filth on the freshly-painted sides, kept busy clambering over the rail into hammocks slung alongside.

When it was my turn, the coxswain thrust me forward, and I ducked my head and entered the captain's cabin of the Hispaniola for the first time since I was a boy. The cabin area, at the stern of the ship, had been refitted since I last saw it -- a beautiful little room, with glass all along the stern, dappled dancing gold from the sunlight off the waves, and not a right angle anywhere to be seen, all graceful curves. There were tiny bulwarks forward making space for the squire and the doctor. They were both there observing, seated off to one side, looking dyspeptic. We had all agreed that I should claim no acquaintance with the sea but that I should stay close to the truth and state that I was a taverner's son. There had been some discussion between the conspirators as to whether I could read and write or not. The Doctor and Squire felt a lettered seaman would be too unusual and liable to be remarked upon. I had argued vehemently for literacy; in my naivety, I wished to be able to read books in the hours when not on duty.

Kapitein Jos von Loendersloot was a hatchet-faced, darkhaired man in a black greatcoat far too warm for this weather. I was not introduced to our two observers. His mate asked me questions about my background which I answered in simple language, tugging at my forelock each time.

Laemmers said, in a heavy Dutch-accent, "What is your name?"

"Hawkins. James Hawkins."

"You have seen the poster for this voyage." I nodded. "What can you do aboard this ship?"

"I'm a landsman, sir, but I know some of the sails, and I can pull a rope."

"Line. We call it line. What do you do on the land, Hawkins James Hawkins?"

"My family own a tavern north on the coast."

Laemmers shot a quick glance at the Kapitein. "This means you can cook?"

I said, hastily, "No, no cooking. I mean, I'm terrible. They never used to let me."

The Kapitein motioned me over and grasped my hands in his great horny paw. He looked at my scarred knuckles with a sort of chuckle, then felt my palms and said something in Dutch to the mate. After an exchange, of which I understood not a word, the mate told me the pay and duration of the voyage, planned to be ten to twenty weeks. I was offered employment as a common seaman. The mate offered me a contract and pen and inkwell. I leaned forward and crudely printed my name. The Kapitein grunted and said, in English, "Landsman taverner Hawkins, waister" and dismissed me with a gesture. But before I turned away I saw the Kapitein tip Laemmers a nod and a wink.

Schooner

Hispaniola

Chapter 4.

The Voyage

My intention of remaining inconspicuous was thwarted on the second forenoon after we set sail. As a landsman, no sailor, I had been assigned to the 'waisters', oxen only good for hauling on whichever line the mysterious activity in the shrouds required.

As I stood in indecision as to which line I was to seize, confused by the first mate's inarticulate bellowing in Dutch and bad English, I was struck foully and most forcefully across the back by the bosuns mate, a great Dutch lout named Klagg, (or Klegg). As his arm drew back to strike me again, I naturally knocked the blackguard down. With a roar, he arose and charged at me, whereupon I coolly struck him to the deck again. Someone once wrote folly is youth's handmaiden. The third time was curtailed by the first mate and several seamen. I was made to understand that I was in great trouble. From the look upon his face it was clear I had made an incontrovertible enemy of this Klagg person.

The Kapitein came down from the quarterdeck to his cabin, and I waited near the door as Klagg stood explaining what had happened in a rush of incomprehensible Dutch, shuffling his feet and blowing his bloodied nose. Klagg concluded, and the Kapitein turned to me and said, "Very bad for discipline, Hawkins." Apparently we understood our English on this occasion. "Klagg is bosuns mate and his job is to start the slow hands. What do you have to say about?"

I had decided that a confused truculence was my best course of action. "I'm not slow. This blackguard hit me! If he hits me again, I'll break his ribs!" Perhaps this was laying it on a bit thick, but my blood was still up.

The Kapitein looked slightly amused; the first mate and Klagg looked grim. After a moment the Kapitein said, "Hawkins to the forward crew, he has energy so much, let him climb. Grog stopped one week."

I knew that my reactions must be all of a piece, and immediately protested strongly as to the loss of my grog ration, which of course I detested.

The first mate looked sharply at the Kapitein, who sighed audibly and then said, "Twelve lashes, Sunday next."

As I brushed past Klagg in the doorway of the Captain's cabin, he whispered, in the purest Cockney, "One dark night, mate."

*****

It was several nights later that it happened. I was too exhausted from climbing and too scared of the heights up in the shrouds to give much thought to my impending flogging, which was scheduled for two days hence. As part of the for'ard crew, I had been aloft in the rigging for much of the past few days, learning each spar, sail, line, and shouted command, usually in Dutch. My mind was awash with learning preventer-stays from ratlines, learning the care and feeding of the fore staysail, the dolphin striker. My hands were raw from the lines, my calves and back ached from climbing. The food was coarse and rough, as were my crewmates, whom I simply avoided speaking to. I hadn't washed in days. Thus I was in an exhausted sleep in my sodden bunk in the foc'sle when I became aware that someone, or several someones, had seized me. In the darkness I felt a firm grip on my queue and the undeniable prick of a dirk at my right kidney. From right behind my ear came a deep, rumbling voice, saying, not unkindly, "We noticed you don't talk to no one, cully. You're talkin' tonight."

Oddly, at this moment, I felt rather than heard Miss Lilith Trelawney's voice in my mind, gently chiding.

"We got 'im, bring us a glim," a rough voice called. A lanthorn was lit and brought up to my bunk, which was surrounded by my beloved crewmates. I recognised the very large, tattooed forearm around my throat as belonging to an enormous seaman nicknamed Yellow Jack; a short, balding, redheaded tough named Sam Dresser stood before me. The Dutch crew members, roused by the light, watched the Englanders from their swaying hammocks with a marked lack of curiosity. I might survive, or I might not.

"Orright, Hawkins," (he pronounced it 'Orkins') "you've some talking to do. About a fortnight ago, some of the lads seen yer down the docks, takin' in the sights of Bristol, calm as you please."

I answered boldly, "What of it? I was searching for a berth."

"Ah, dressed in bleedin' gentleman's finery? Dick, come up here."

A huge, shy creature, Dick had a roundish, moon face and the body of a bull. He stared at the deck, at the faces around us, a smelly, dirty group to be sure, everywhere but at me. I could hear the working of the hull as water hissed and thumped at the sides, tumbling from the bows.

Sam Dresser cried impatiently, "Dick, tell us what ye saw."

"I saw this'n walkin' about Bristol, in and out 'o taverns. I saw 'im three or four times."

Sam frowned. "His dress! How was he dressed?"

Dick's speech rose slowly, as if from a great distance. "He's wearin'.. a green frock coat wif lace at the cuffs, and white leggings, and a ribbon in 'is queue, and.." he trailed off into silence.

I was impressed at this creature's powers of observation, and wished him roasting on a spit. Sam Dresser turned to me and brought his face quite near mine. The missing teeth were a charming complement to his ruddy, unshaven cheeks. I reflected he had had the scurvy in a past voyage; it was common in those days before mariners, always a backwards lot, finally took notice of James Lind's excellent 1753 treatise on 'Treatment Of The Scurvy'.

"And who exactly might ye be, young gentleman, and why are ye dressed in sailcloth like us? Ye're no Dutchman, can't be the Kapitein's man -- Are ye the King's spy?

Ye're some sort of spy -- why are you here ?" He pulled a foot-long dirk, and brandishing it at me, hissed, "Quick now, or it's over the side for ye." The disembodied arm tightened around my neck, while the crew's shadows lurched about crazily.

My mind had been racing from his first accusation. I bitterly regretted not stopping outside Bristol and buying coarser clothing, in disguise from the outset. Instead I'd maundered all over town still dressed as a young Oxford gentleman. I had supposed that appearing thus would exempt me from the press gangs, which it had. Foolish schoolboy. How to explain appearing in expensive gentlemen's finery, and escape a dunking or death ?

My imagination was lent wings, spurred on, no doubt, by the bite of the knife at my back, as I began to save my life. As composedly as one could, with an arm around one's throat, I said, "Do any of you lot know what entail and primogeniture are?"

Silence for a moment, then one, a meagre, longhaired seaman named Allan said, "Ay. Me Da had a farm County Cork way; I'm the third brother. Me oldest brother is the farmer now, me next brother is now the Father." He grinned at this witticism.

"That's the way of it," another hand in back said. "The eldest gets the land, the rest gets the back o'me hand."

"It's not just custom, lads, it's the King's law," I went on. In for a penny, in for a pound. "The law exists so family estates don't get cut into ever-smaller parcels as generations pass. And like Allan's family and mine, the firstborn son inherits everything and the rest go in the

Army, become clergy, apprentice somewhere, or go to sea."
I looked around. "Like us."

I went on to describe my childhood as the son of a second
son of a great house; the law required that my uncle
inherit everything. Living apart from the estate, son of a
simple taverner (true). First my father died (true) and
then the eldest brother passed on; encouraged by my
mother, I attempted to locate and assume my birthright,
only to find my father's evil younger brother had occupied
and controlled the estate.

Looking around, I realised I had them. Listening in the
near-dark, they huddled, waiting for the rest, knives
lowered. Continuing, emphasising my youth and
inexperience, I described how I had gone to the local
magistrate and attempted to hire a solicitor, with my
meagre resources; rebuffed, I had nowhere to turn. My
voice lowered, I told how my uncle, unbeknownst to me,
had been deeply alarmed; I described how I was abducted,
tied and flung into a waggon, and loaded onto a ship
headed out to sea. They looked at each other, nodding
significantly. Sailors love a good yarn. The arm about my
throat had loosened appreciably.

I went on and said, "And so, lads, I was aboard, had to
work in the waist or be thrown overboard. A wild
Scotsman, a swordsman of repute, befriended me. It was
winter. Off the coast of Scotland, we escaped, and had
many adventures in Scotland before my friend was re-
established with his family and his birthright. He gave me
a very small amount of money, which I would be happy to
share, and one suit of fine clothes, which you, Dick, have
seen me in. But the introductions to the aristocracy in
Bristol did not work out; and so I took this berth, here on

the Hispaniola. What say you? Should I be killed for trying to make my way ? Well, lads?"

It was apparent throughout that I quite knew my audience. Their instinctive dislike of the gentry was the linchpin of my performance; and no one could blame a disenfranchised young man for trying to rise in the world. So I was not surprised to see the crewmen, eyes glistening, give a Huzzah! and cry, "Hear him! Hear him!" and "Hurrah for Gentleman Jim!" and "Double shares for Mister Jim!" (for there was much treasure-talk among the hands) and set me free, clapping me on the shoulders and back. Large, cruel boys, really, and as gullible, liking a good story. For perhaps the first time, though not the last, I reflected the advantage my mind gave me over much of humanity.   Dirk sheathed, Sam Dresser thrust his hand toward me, and I shook it firmly.

When things quieted down, Sam Dresser stepped to the door of the foc'sle cabin, and gestured to me to come on deck with him.   Out on the windy deck, in the dim lamplight coming forward from the quarterdeck, Sam Dresser whispered to me. "Verra pretty spoke. On'y you and I know it's a great pack o'lies."

I was stunned.   "You're daft.   Every word's the God's truth."

Dresser grinned at me.   "Oh, aye.. the Kapitein and Laemmers have your number, laddie - friend and 'confidante' of the owners, that Doctor an' Squire. Kapitein told me an' Klagg to ride you, hard."

Wollett the solicitor, no doubt, had met with the Kapitein and mentioned me.   For once my gift of gab had deserted.

"But don't worry," said Dresser, " - wot they don't know is I hate a Dutchman, and I like you - you're fast on yer feet, like me. Our secret, eh?" And he clapped me on the shoulder in the friendliest way. From that day forward, the entire English-speaking crew called me "the young guv'nor" or "Mr Jim". From that day forward, they were mine.

While at work on deck next day, holystoning and swabbing, I caught a snatch of conversation behind me about pirates. Pricking up my ears, I mopped closer to two of the mainsail hands, sitting on the hatch cover picking oakum. One of them was saying, "... and they comes in a barky called Teredo. You mind the Teredo, Jock?" The other, a villainous, tattooed skeleton, possibly deaf from too many broadsides, absently replied, "Ay. A town in Spain, innit?" Smiling, I slowly mopped myself away, whistling 'Lillibullero' for old King James.

While Livesey occasionally appeared on the quarterdeck, this week I had seen nothing whatever of Trelawney; I reflected spitefully that the great sailor might be prostrate below with the sea-sickness. I must own that the Squire was correct in one thing: the unladen Hispaniola, with its schooner rigging, scraped hull and shallow draft, was remarkably fast. The second mate, who had dropped the log, said to the coxswain in heavily accented English, "Nine knots before the wind"; if my shipmates were to be believed, men-of-war wallowed along at six to seven knots; light frigates were lucky to make nine or ten. There were two eighteen-pound cannon aboard, and two heavy carronades, useful only for close-range bombardment. So our role was to be hare, not hound.

Later that same day, with a rare moment to myself, I leaned against the rail amidships, looking at the grey-green sea, thinking idly of my graduation and impending medical practice, the delicate state of being a gentleman, and treasure. Most especially I thought of Miss Bellingham, who had taken the news of my voyage most gracelessly, and of her father, an obstinate defender of the sanctity of the privileged.

I opened and reread a letter received in Bristol; it had a tiny, diffident preface in an immature hand:

"Dear James, I am so much agitated that I can scarce hold a pen. I am sensible that I have exposed myself to a Situation beyond my Forbearance."

The letter fluttered in the sea-breeze as I read on. No more Ever Amiable, I reflected. A girl from a less profitable concern would be chagrined at letting a ten-thousand-pounder slip away.

Allan sidled up to me, tow in hand, and asked, "Letter from a lady?"

"Aye," I said moodily. "The wrong one." I opened my hand and watched the joyless little note float away.

Sunday dawned clear and clean. The British crew in the foc'sle were clumsily solicitous to me all morning. Several of the hands had noted that the Kapitein had me working right up to Sunday morning, rather than confining me below. Though it kept my mind and body occupied, working aloft could easily have been a death sentence, falling on deck or in the ocean. The Dutch ignored me as usual. After we broke our fast, the coxswain came for me.

The ship's company were loosely scattered about the deck, looking sullen, even the Dutchmen. I could hear Dresser crying, "Come now, don't scatter like a flock of gammy birds, to the waist." My silent sentries stripped me of my shirt and fastened a kind of leather apron over my lower back, meant to protect the kidneys. Klagg, holding a cat-o-nine, had a smirk on his face. His nose was still a sort of purple.

Lashed to a grating leaned against the mainmast, I noted how curiously absorbing and visually interesting the wood grain in the grate had become. The colours and shades were worthy of a master painter, like the sea frozen in time, endlessly fascinating. A whole world of whorls, if only I had time to view it. Of course this strange, silent interlude was interrupted quite rudely. It would be difficult not to attribute some personal animosity to the assiduity with which Klagg the bosuns mate wielded the cat. The crew, assembled in the waist, looked on impassively or sullenly. While my back was an agony, I was gratified to note that I did not cry out. Twelve I could bear; the hands said that the Royal Navy dispensed hundreds of lashes for similar offences to mine; this was nothing in comparison.

As I was helped belowdecks, I was touched to see that several of the British hands came to me with a pail of grog; they had foregone their grog rations so that "Mr Jim could have the dose" for my pain. Wanting a clear head, I asked the hands to keep it for me until after my meeting with Dr Livesey. We continued down to see the Doctor, set up with a wash, salve and bandages in the small cubby called the orlop. Tom and Eben, the two hands that had propelled me into the orlop, left me there.

Livesey eyed me. "Well, Hawkins, I know it is difficult to arrange a private meeting on a small ship; however, another method might have saved the skin on your back.

I apologise for not interceding on your behalf; as owner I could have done. But your anonymity would have been at an end. Sit here. That fellow Klagg has it 'in for you', as the sailors say." The Doctor took up his wash and began.

"I'm far from anonymous, Doctor - the Kapitein and Laemmers have told Klagg and one of the British crew that I'm a 'spy for the owners'."

Livesey said, "Wollett, right?"

I nodded. "Must have been."

To distract myself I looked around this small cabin, a doctor's office, really, with a locked cupboard for palliatives and space for three hammocks; sprains and rupture were common with men being used as bullocks. "Doctor, we can't make it back to Bristol in thirty days. Can't you press the Kapitein to set more sail?"

"I have. He refuses, on the grounds this is an old unsound vessel. Don't forget who he works for. We may not be meant to return in time. Tell me, what is the mood and disposition of the crew?"

"Doctor, every living soul aboard excepting the livestock is intensely aware that this is a treasure voyage. The English foc'sle hands discuss the finding and distribution of the treasure interminably. Sir, that hurts. No outright mutiny or methods of seizure have been discussed in my hearing. For all love, could you treat another area for a bit?" I thought for a moment. "The hands blithely ignore the fact that none of us has been promised a share, and ignore that the putative purpose of this voyage is trade; I fear they will prove intractable indeed should we have to shift or load cargo... unless it were treasure. Give way, there, another spot, I beg you."

"I am not one given to stories," said the Doctor, still working away behind me, "But I am reminded of the fellow who wanted a tattoo of a great British lion on his back. The tattooist began, and in a moment the fellow was saying, oh, oh, stop, what is that you're doing? The lion's back, your Honour, said the tattooist. Move on, I say, do another part, said the fellow. In another moment the fellow is crying stop, what is that part? The tail, your Honour. Well, give way, do elsewhere. Sure enough, in moments the fellow is crying out again, oh, oh, what is that part you're doing? The tattooist said, the lion's mane, your Honour, and I quit - whoever heard of a lion with no back, tail, or mane?" He hurhurred for a moment, pleased with his wit at my expense.

Hoho, indeed. Unsmilingly, I asked, "Should you like to know more of the crew?"

"Certainly. Are any of the crew more likely to turn than others? Are there any leaders?"

"There are two natural leaders among the British," I said. "One, Sam Dresser, short, red-faced..." The Doctor murmured in recognition. I continued, "Dresser appears a dockside blowhard, something of a sea-lawyer, with an abiding grudge against the upper classes." Wincing from his ministrations to my back, I went on, "And there's another to watch out for. You've noticed a tall blonde fellow about sixteen stone, heavily tattooed? The hands call him Yellow Jack -- as for the Dutch, they're a mystery to me. I assume they follow the first mate's lead."

I flexed my shoulders experimentally, which was a painful mistake. "And of course I've an enemy in the bosuns mate. Don't know how much influence the fellow has." It occurred to me that I could have cheerfully murdered Klagg in any of a thousand ways. On the heels of this was the thought that some of my newfound acolytes among the British crew would cheerfully do the deed as well.

Dr Livesey looked thoughtful. "We've done what we can regarding mutiny, stowed all the arms in the locker near the great cabin..." He fell silent, musing, as I slowly and painfully pulled on my shirt.   He sent me back to my duty, my newfound chums, and my unwelcome pail of rum.   I had begun to get quite used to it.   On my way out the door, he called after me, "Your back should be fine in a week.   Just avoid undue stretching and exertion."

Chapter 5.

Impressed

Late afternoon a week later, stiff but game, I was out on the plunging bowsprit, clinging for dear life, with the for'ard crew, working, I understood, to re-rig the flying jib to the foremast. I was told that "blasted, lazy swabs" at the shipyard had concealed rotten rigging beneath a coat of fresh tar. One of the British crew, a young idiot named Allard, who professed to love heights, was lookout that day. Unexpectedly, his excited call, almost a squeak, came from aloft, "Sail ho!".   A pause; an octave lower: "Sail ho!".

"Where away?" shouted the bosun.

A pause, "Larboard astern, hull-down. Angling across our wake." Consternation among the for'ard crew; we'd just stripped down the flying jib's rigging, robbing the Hispaniola of an important sail. We became very busy. The first mate bolted for the stern, toward the captain's cabin and the arms locker. All hands were piped on deck. Moments later the Kapitein came thudding up the stairs to the quarterdeck, carrying his long telescope. Allard called down again, "She's changed course for us, still hull-down. Square-rigged, sir!" Hoarse commands punctuated the plash from the bows and the creaking of the rigging.

The coxswain came forward and began a series of rapid-fire commands in excited Dutch and mangled Shakespearean English, and over the next hour we completed rigging a temporary dolphin striker under the bowsprit, spray from the plunging bows soaking us to the skin, stinging my back like nettles. We finished the replacement rigging from the foremast to the bowsprit as the rest of the crew hung all available canvas. My sodden clothes grew chill as the breeze freshened. A small gunnery crew sanded the deck and stacked shot for our few cannon. One of the gun crew cried aloud in Dutch, ending in the English word "stern-chaser!" as he trundled shot along the deck. I gathered he wanted one.

Kapitein von Loendersloot's back was to the crew for a long while as he observed our apparent pursuer. Our square-rigged company was still on our course, hull down over the horizon, as we were to them. The main boom barely cleared the captain's head as we tacked, changing course to due south. The race was on.

A whispered conference, and the bosun appeared from below bearing a large folded flag. I heard one of the foretop crew say to another, "No, mate, it ain't yellow, and the Yellow Jack won't work, see, our course is all wrong. Ye don't get sick from the Jack 'til the tropics, not fresh from England like us. And flyin' the flag won't help - some 'o these privateers'll sink a plague ship, just for the gunnery practice."

The old Hispaniola, resplendent in a new suit of sail in the bright sunlight, heeled over so far that the lee rail was buried in foam. The Kapitein climbed aloft with his telescope, the better to observe our companion. Hands crept along the waist holding lines strung between the masts. Above on the creaking foremast crosstree awaiting further sail-handling orders, I looked straight down and saw only water rushing by. Dizzy, I quickly turned to see our pursuer's sails. Still hull down. Were we pulling away? In the bows below me, the second mate dropped the log. Moments later we heard his hoarse shout, "Twelve knots one fathom." I saw the hands nodding approvingly and tipping one another the wink. One of the hands aloft, I could not see who, shouted, "Hoy, mate, we're truly cracking on!"

A further set of commands led to all hands aloft, running additional braces and stays to stabilise the two masts, which were creaking and bending alarmingly. The schooner, plunging wildly ahead, heeled over sharply, did its best to buck us off, far above deck, far above the grey-green water. Any hand losing his grip would likely drown; even if the fall did not stun him, he was unlikely to know how to swim. Under chase, the ship was not going to stop for a man overboard. "One hand for the ship, the other hand for your life," as the hands said. The crews were called down to the deck, and half went below for a hurried meal. A young maintopman nicknamed Mersey (from Liverpool, naturally) told me that we'd likely be clear if we could stay loose until nightfall; a moonless night and an unexpected change of course should prove us free in the morning. The lookouts reported the square-rigger still hull-down, not gaining.

Below, while eating, discussion among the hands revealed plenty of motives for running; while all other seafaring nations, it seemed, were at war with England, one of the worst fates to befall us would be to be stopped and boarded by the Royal Navy. As it was wartime, a Navy captain would not cavil at pressing as many of our crew as he needed. So for this voyage, literally every sail represented an enemy.

"No, mate, that ain't it," said the same, well-informed foretopman. "I hear the Capting has a Paper." This caused a bit of whispered talk along the table. Sam Dresser turned to the crewman. "A Paper, you say - what kind of Paper might this be?" The fore crew, known as Fitz, answered, "From Admiralty. All the Capting has to do is show this Paper to a officer, I don't care he's a d____d Royal Navy Commodore, yes, sir, sorry to bother, we're under way again, safe as houses." This was very pleasing to the hands; it was thought a ship with a Paper "mought well have a Lucky Voyage".

Another hand ventured, "I'll wager that's why we had no visits from the press in Harbour. I'd like to see that gang boss and say, 'Fie on your press - we've got a Paper.'" And he shook his fist. This sally was met with much admiration.

A sudden, "'All hands on deck!'" came from above, and we scrambled up on the deck of the plunging, sharply heeled ship. Whilst we were eating it had turned full dark. As I emerged the Doctor darted forward and pulled me aside to the taffrail for a hasty whispered consultation. "Jim, I've been listening to the officers -- they think it's the Americans. I dare not keep the map on me, nor is it safe to secret it in the ship. You keep it. I must stay below with Trelawney -- he is still quite ill." He handed me a waxed sailcloth packet, and repeated the latitude and longitude of the island to me several times.

I could hear the bosun shouting for me to come forward. "Doctor, what good is the map? Ben Gunn moved it all, and the bearings are not on it any more."

He shook his head. "Keep it. I cannot. In its own way it's quite valuable. It may buy your life." Puzzled, I thrust the map in my shirtwaist and ran for'ard.

I do not propose to bore the reader with the endless sail-handling of that long night; indeed, I understood so little sailing arcana that that it was a blur of climbing, holding on, and pulling until my hands bled; suffice it to say that we changed our course from South to due East into the teeth of the wind, hoping to shake our pursuer in the dark. Endless commands streamed from the quarterdeck, and the hands worked with a will, squeezing every bit of speed possible, until we split a topsail. I was sent below to roust up a spare, in the wee hours of the morning, with only a few dim lanthorns in the hold; we tried to wrestle this infuriatingly limp and heavy roll of canvas up from its resting-place and finally, bathed in sweat, we had it on deck, still canted steeply over, lee rail still swamped. The top crew were ready, and speedily grappled the sail into its rightful place.

All hands were still on deck as dawn began to break. It was a glorious sight, black fading to indigo, made less so by the sight of the white sails of our square-rigged pursuer, only a couple of miles off. I understood they "had the weather-gauge" of us, and that the game was up.

Schooner

Hispaniola

Part II. - THE REVENGE

Chapter 6.

The Americans

I once read an account by Tacitus regarding Roman galley slaves during a sea battle. Chained in place, unable to see what was happening abovedecks, lashed to exhaustion, the rowers had no chance of escape should their ship be sunk or, worse, burnt.

The Hispaniola's crew were rowed across to the American ship, a frigate named "Revenge", herded below at bayonet-point, a group at a time, down steep stairs, through a gun deck with guns manned, portholes open. One of our hands behind me muttered, "Eighteen-pounders."

A call came dimly from the topdeck, "Sail Ho! hull up, to windward!" The last group of us came trooping down and then the bluecoated sentries hurriedly dragged the hatch cover into place, plunging the hold into darkness.

Sam Dresser, who was among this last group, said, "It's a British man-o'war they've sighted - she's close - they'll be under way." We then heard a flurry of shouted orders, feet thudding overhead, the groan of lines in tackle, followed with the tilt and sway of the deck.

The sharp-eyed lookout, Allard, added, "A three-deck seventy-four, it was."

The Dutch and British crew sat in a ragged circle on the deck and on the crates lashed into the hold, and held an impromptu council in the dark. I could hear the rustling and chittering of rats behind me in the darkness, very quiet. A Dutch sailor, a Jan something, asked if the Kapitein, the officers, and the owners (meaning Trelawney and Livesey) had been brought aboard the rebel ship before it began to move. Consensus seemed to be that the officers and owners had been detained in the Kapitein's cabin in the Hispaniola whilst we were brought over to the American ship under guard, in two groups.

Next to me Allan offered, "Small crew for a frigate."

Sam Dresser stated, "This ain't no rebel ship - this here's a Royal Navy Frigate, lads, out of Portsmouth, I wager, and I wonder how these ragtags took her." This was followed by a reflective silence.

"Mebbe that seventy-four won't fire on us, thinkin' His Majesty aboard," said Allard the lookout.

Off in the dark, Yellow Jack rumbled, "Sam, you're mighty up on bleedin' frigates and Navy shipyards and the like. Is there a 'run' next your name somewheres?"

"Belay that, matey, I sailed wi' Hawke's squadron and I got me affydavy on't," cried Sam Dresser.

Brighouse, one of the landlubbers who fancied himself something of a tough, asked, "How far below are we? I can't swim."

"Below the waterline, mate," said Jack, "the only thing under us," (here he stamped on the deck) "is the bilges. Listen—" Above us we could hear thumps and sharp cries. "That'll be the gunports closin' - I think she's running." We sat and listened, and it seemed to me the rebel ship was indeed changing course. Above our heads the heavy cannons rolled into position in their trucks.

Allan said, "Aye, she is, no problem outrunning a seventy-four. What was that?" We could hear a deep thud coming through the very sides of the ship.

"Bow-chasers on the seventy-four, coming through the water," said Sam Dresser, "and if they're good they can cut up her rigging or maybe get a mast. We might hear some return fire from this lot." Chasers, it appeared, were cannon mounted on the bow or stern of a warship, used only during pursuit. "When I was with Admiral Hawke, lads," said Sam -- here many of the crew groaned in mock-anguish— "I was on the Indomitable and we chased the Frenchies, a seventy-four, and the bow-chasers got her right in the rudder— the gun crew got ten quid each right from the Captain."

From my far left came, "Right, mate, I heard you was on the Sally, out of Liverpool, running calico." Snickers all around, cut short by two thudding cracks, very loud above us (for we were far astern in the ship), the rebel stern-chasers returning fire.

A few minutes later came the sound of the rebel's crew cheering from above. Sam Dresser grunted, "Must've got a mast on our three-decker --- " and there came a smash and rush of water from the stern. "We're for it, boys," shouted

Sam, "she's hulled— we're trapped!" The British gun-crew had the range, for two or three more shots smashed into our stern, and the rushing sound of water grew louder. The rats began to squeak and chitter all around us.

I stood, more from nervousness than a sense of command. "Jack, Brighouse, you lot, let's see how secure these hatches are. See if you can find a board or something to push or pry with." Above the stern-chasers continued to fire as fast as they could, about once per minute, perhaps less.

Yellow Jack said, "Let me try first," and climbed the narrow stairs to the hatch cover. I could hear him grunt and push at the cover. If any one of the crew was suited for this task, it was the giant Jack.

From above came a rending crash, and the ship slewed around sideways. In the dark, one of the hands shouted, "Got a mast or summat!" We heard the sharp creak of the gunports opening and the rumble of the cannons on the gundeck above. The deck below us was awash in water, and rats squeaked and dropped into the water all around us. Our crew began to climb up on the crates, pushing and shoving at the hatch cover. Allard cried out on my left, "Rat-bite !" and flung something soft away with an oath. The rebels fired a ragged broadside from the gundeck above. I had never heard a sound so loud -- I thought my ears would burst. It was followed by a second broadside from the top gundeck. I heard Yellow Jack call to someone off in the darkness, "Broadsides with a seventy-four - it's suicide."

My case was floating free now, bobbing about and bumping against stanchions. A rat climbed my back, and I writhed around on the case to get it, and the whole lot rolled over in the dark, flinging me off. The water was over our heads now, hands screaming, holding onto the rails of the stairway, treading water.

"She's turning away," cried Allard, and indeed we could feel the ship leaning into the wind, and I could dimly hear the rebels cheering on the gundeck above. I had wedged myself up into a corner, but by this time the rats were climbing on our shoulders, arms, and clawing their way up on my face and in my hair, squealing in terror of drowning. The water was within a foot of the roof of the hold, and men were screaming for rescue in their own languages, talking to their mothers, to their God. Breathing so hard and fast I thought I would faint, I lost my purchase in my corner and was treading water in the dark, alert for floating cases nearby, brushing rats off my head, trying to orient on the hatch cover.

Someone shouted "She's down by the stern - go forward!" I splashed through the dark water and indeed farther forward in the hold, there was more space between the water and the planking above.

Cannon fire, except for the chasers immediately above us, had ceased entirely. One of the crew had resumed pounding on the underside of the hatch. The waters, the filthy, stinking bilge-waters, continued to rise. I believed any death would be better than this, trapped like rodentia, drowning in the dark, screaming crew all around me; a body bumped me, floating facedown, and with my free hand I grasped its collar, lifting the face and head out of the water. I shook the heavy body like a terrier, and was rewarded with a gasping cough and the sound of vomiting. "Thanks, cully," said Yellow Jack.

Behind me, there was a sudden light - we were rescued ! The crew swarmed toward the hatch, lined with rebels, peering at us, bobbing in the water with the rats. "Come up outta that," said   a tenor voice with a harsh, nasal accent.   The last few to emerge were quiet indeed: three Dutchmen and one Briton had drowned in the darkness.

The Hispaniolas now numbered   nine Britons and four Dutchmen, shivering and dripping on the rebel's gundeck. The gundeck was a shambles, guns dismounted, huge holes in the ship's sides, blood, a few bodies stacked toward the stern, soon joined by the wet bodies from our crew, already cold to the touch and inhumanly heavy.   Ship's carpenters laden with tools hastened into the hold we had just left, with lines tied around their waists.   Screaming came from far forward - screaming very familiar to me.   The ship's surgeon must have hit bone with his saw.

A short, blond man in a blue uniform remarkably similar to a British Lieutenant's stood before us.   "Right - I'm Lieutenant Tom McCully.   This ship is taking on water at over a foot a minute.   You will pump watch and watch until we empty the hold."   His pale blue eyes darted back and forth along our shambling line.   His voice was hoarse, louder than normal - no doubt he was slightly deafened by the cannon.   He was filthy, bleeding onto his own feet, and his freckled moon face, which looked like it was normally a cheerful ruddy colour, was pale beneath the grime and smoke smears.   He continued, "Any man deserting his place for any reason will be shot.   To the pumps, Hispaniolas."

Three Marines with fixed bayonets herded us toward the stern.   Behind me I heard McCully say to someone, "D__n right I mean it— a third of the crew dead, a third wounded, and the ship's settling ever' minute.   Get the for'ard pump going! All right, good, KEEP it going!"

If ever I meet the person who designed and installed the pumps in that ship, he will be dead in moments.   A more contrary invention would be impossible to create.   Black iron and brass, the pump stood in the centre of a sort of frame-work or treadle similar to the pumps on fire-engines. Except these handles, instead of being shoulder or even waist-high, were situated near the deck, so that one either sat on the deck or performed a sort of unending obeisance, like a Hindoo Faqir. The first hour warmed us up and loosened us up from our cold immersion in the hold. We even had enough breath to talk to one another at first; I was stationed across from Dresser and Allan, who looked ready to collapse. Within another hour, he did collapse, to be dragged to the side by a Marine, who grimly took his place. There was hammering all over the ship, including, I imagined, a crew trying to patch the shot-holes below the waterline.

Above us, I gathered, were men attempting to piece together enough rigging and working sails to get more than steerage-way. The light from the topdeck above faded, and one small lanthorn was brought back to us. A few of the eighteen-pound balls, freed in some mishap during the broadsides, rolled about, threatening ankles and feet, until the Marines gave permission for us to secure them. There was a similar crew, we were told, being worked beyond exhaustion far forward, fighting the sea. We pumped until we collapsed in place, dragged out of the way, left alone for a while, then forced back to the pumps with bayonet-prods from the Marines, who, to their credit, worked right alongside of us, muskets laid on the deck. We worked all that night, only a piggin of ale for all of us. Above we heard a ragged, wheezy cheer. Dresser gasped, "She's riding higher now, they must've plugged her."

Indeed, we were let off the pumps one by one, to collapse out of the way, in amongst the great cannon. Beneath an open gunport letting in the grey predawn light, I curled up, making certain my sailcloth packet was still secure, and fell asleep with the clank and wheeze of the pumps in my ears.

A Marine prodded me awake, motioning to a mug of water and some biscuit. I attacked it, looking around me. It was full day, and the pumps were still going, but manned by only three men a side. Jan the Dutchman was on the other side of one of my cannon. Grinning widely, showing a mouthful of biscuit, he gestured at the hatch to the hold. "Glad to be living!" he said, raising his mug in a toast.

I stood, stiffly, and asked one of the Marines the way to the seat of ease. He pointed me forward, and I walked along the gundeck, looking at the damage. The ship was pitching gently, only making three or four knots, sunbeams swinging back and forth. It appeared this ship was again headed due south, toward the friendly ports of Spanish America. The deck was drying from having being swabbed, and the powder bags and shot had all been shifted back to the magazine, I imagined. Most of the damage was on one side, though the other had the occasional hole where shot had passed right through the ship. Some of the portholes had been beaten into shapeless gouges, and several of the cannon were still on their sides, ropes snapped, shifting uneasily as the deck tilted. The carpenters were still pounding away above and below. I passed the forward pumps, with four men working them. A sailor moved toward me, hand on his dirk, but I forestalled him by jerking my thumb forward.

On my way back toward the stern, a crew of five rebel sailors were working with marline-spikes and crowbars to shift one of the cannon, a hulking great black thing on its side, weighing several tons. They had it almost over when it slipped, a large wood sliver catching one of the men behind the knee, slicing into the popliteal artery, which started to spurt blood wildly with every heartbeat. It took only a split second to decide a course of action which would get me off the pumps. I leapt at the leg, digging my thumb in above the wound, and snapped at the sailor I took to be the leader, "Give me some cloth and a small stick." One of the hands ran forward and returned in a moment with a dirty strip of linen and a large splinter from the ship's sides. Working quickly, I tourniqueted the place and told the men to hold the stick while they carried him to the surgeon. It happened very quickly, and I spoke with such assurance that none of the sailors even questioned me.

It was back to the aft pumps for me; never a sight of blue sky, little air, stale and foul, and we toiled by the hour to gain on the sea. After five or six cycles of collapsing at the pumps, being revived with bread and water, I began to think of escape, a ludicrous but involving enterprise. Perhaps I could, under cover of darkness, steal a ship's boat, lower it from its davits by myself without being seen or heard, or perhaps if I climbed high enough in the rigging and jumped for it, on the way down I could learn to fly. Lt McCully made several appearances, each time looking cleaner and more military, only speaking to the marine guard, never to the prisoners.

I wondered how Livesey and the Squire were faring. A bit of conversation with Sam Dresser and Allan made us reckon there were eight left aboard the Hispaniola: Doctor and Squire, von Loendersloot, Jan Laemmers the first mate, van der Heijden the bosun, Klagg the bosun's mate, the second mate and the coxswain. "No worries, Jim, it'll be all hands, not easy, but they're provisioned," said Allan. "Sail around the world, they could."

Over time, American crewmembers were directed to join us as the pumps. As breath allowed, and over our quick meals, their story emerged. One seaman, almost Jack's size, named Seale, seemed willing to talk. Typically, it was Dresser who asked, "Matey, might you tell us how you Americans took this here frigate clean away from His Majesty's Navy?"

Seale grinned and said, "Aye, it were McCully. Month ago, late in't day we seen a sail hull down leeward. We got close enow t' see the Union Jack before darkness fell. The Lootenant, he went to Cap'n Gus with a plan. We took a longboat with our longest light line, padded the oars, used one sail, and sailed right up her stern. T'were pitch dark, no stars. We had one line back to the cutter, and t'other end in hand." Seale paused, considering. "McCully, he took the line and jumped for the rudder, and tied on to the rudder-pintles. T'other two boats followed the line. We all climbed up the stern, quiet as Indians, knocked the afterguard on the head, and had the hatch covers on in a minute. The Royals had the gun-deck, right, so Revenge stayed astern, but we had the ship.   It took a day of smoke-bombs down the hatches before they all surrendered, mates, and it were a joy to behold.   We packed all the Navy boys belowdecks on the old Revenge, sent her back t' Dunkirk, and renamed this'n. Whatever ship Cap'n Conyngham is on is the Revenge."

Two days or so went by, perhaps less. I was in a dreamless sleep curled up between the cannon, braced against the hull, when a kick on my foot wakened me. A thin, harassed-looking powder boy was standing next to a marine. The marine said, "Go with Connor here and do what you're told." Without a word, the youngster, no more than eight or ten years old, grasped me by the sleeve and tugged me forward through the gundeck and up a small stairs. The boy deposited me in front of a door, which he rapped upon, and left me.

A tall, thin, grey, very weary man in a bloody smock opened the door and motioned me in. Looking me up and down, he said, "So you're the surgeon, huh? How'd you learn to tourniquet and stop bleeding? I'm Dr Monroe, by the way."

At last. Only two days of pumping late. "Which I was loblolly boy for that Dr Livesey on Hispaniola, sir."

"We ain't been to Hispaniola Isle," he said.

"Not the island, sir, I come from that little schooner whose crew you pressed a few days ago. I can grind compounds and give physick, your Honour."

He gave a short laugh, like a bark. "Physick— don't need it. We have good salt pork and horse not above twenty years old, from the French war. Cleans 'em out like a sluice-pipe. But the boys I have helping me are all bumblers. I need a helper." He looked at me slyly and said, "Unless you enjoy the pumps. We have to pump all the way to the next port, could be a week of pumping, I shouldn't wonder. Your name?"

I was done with that accursed pump forever, with this man's help. Escape comes in many forms. "Hate pumping, your Honour. Happy to nurse here. Uh, Jim Hawkins."

"Belay your Honour. Call me Dr Monroe. Let's go."

The very front of the gundeck was closed off, making, as I found, a sick-bay and operating-room. It was crammed with swaying hammocks, with lanthorns every few feet, not lit during the day. This area had its own two gunports (though no cannon), open to the light and sea-breeze in clement weather, with an occasional spray coming up and in; sticking my head out, I noted that I could easily drop into the sea, once the ship was anchored.

Dr Monroe was a sort of country doctor-sur-mer. But he was also, when rested a bit, a good conversationalist, and loved to sound me out about my British views of the American Revolution, as he called it, naming himself and the men aboard Patriots and citizens of a new nation. He declaimed, "And that is why the motto on this ship's flag says, 'United Now Alive and Free Firm on this Basis Liberty Shall Stand and Thus Supported Ever Bless Our Land Till Time Becomes Eternity'".

I made myself surly and taciturn, and named him 'rebel' to his face, which he smiled and shrugged off, moving on to the next memorised and closely-reasoned tract from Thomas Paine. Common sense, indeed.

I settled in to a sick-bay routine only slightly less exhausting than pumping, because of the number of badly wounded hands, and the different types of care needed. Once again catching short naps curled in a corner, at least I ate better, with the sick, and fed them too, and collected their slops, and indeed ground compounds. I also espied a perfect cache for Flint's map, which had long chafed the skin on my back. I wondered how Yellow Jack and Dresser and Allan and the rest were faring. Pumped to shadows, I suspected.

Night followed day, marked off by the ship's bells. One of the surgeries explained the bell-system to me; basically they were rung, and watches changed, every four hours, except the first and last dogs, which were only two hours long. Kapitein von Loendersloot had employed a much more humane policy of eight hour watches, except when it was all hands on deck.

There was much banter between the patients regarding the lost Hispaniola; puzzlement as to why she carried no cargo, and detailed calculations as to how much she'd have brought as a prize in Spanish America, divided between the hands according to rank and head-count. Sailors being sailors, their minds then ran on to the pleasures which money and a friendly port would bring. To hear them, they never saved anything, and were usually restored to the ship in a barrow and sling, being unable to walk. "I'd have had a fine old time in Port au-Prince with that 2 pound 10, I would," said one.

Chapter 7.

The Chase

A few days later word came that a sail had been sighted. With the likelihood of action, Dr Monroe and I lashed together two sea-chests with a fairly clean sail cover, as an operating table. He set me to touching up the scalpels and saws, while I listened to the sea-talk of my invalids, who seemed both greatly enlivened at the prospect of action, and cast down because of their imprisonment in the sick-bay.

A Marine announced, "The Captain!" and one half second later in swept Captain Gustavus Conyngham, a tall, thin man with a tanned, drawn face and aristocrat's hands. Our patients had begun writhing about in their hammocks, either to stand muster or to present a cleaner, more military appearance. Joseph Bandy, gunner, missing a left forearm, stood stiffly at attention. Conyngham's face softened as he said, "At ease, Gunny, this isn't your fight today." he turned away from the gunner and said, "At any rate, lads, it looks like a blackbirder, and we have the weather-gauge. It looks good. Are any of these men able to man their stations, Doctor?"

Monroe's face was a study. I thought he wanted to shout the Captain out of the sick-bay, to protect his patients; on the other hand, prize was this ship's reason for being, and a slaver was a cash prize. The Captain did soon go away, taking a fast-healing chest splinter wound, and a torn calf muscle, well-bound, leaving several others in varying stages of distress. A few, of course, were too far gone to care.

I wasn't about to go through a second engagement locked belowdecks without at least being able to see; I and two of the more ambulatory men prevailed on the Doctor to allow us to leave the leeward port gunport open until broadsides appeared likely. We could see the slaver on the horizon, almost stern on. They explained that having the 'weather-gauge' meant we were upwind of our prey; that is, the wind was passing from us to them. This meant the Revenge could decide whether and when to engage. One of my companions, a Bob Fea, noted that the slaver didn't appear to have all its sails. Indeed, as we closed over time (we ate our meagre dinner at the gunport) it was clear that our rate of sail quite outpaced hers, and the other sailor confidently predicted an engagement within the next hour.

"If'n a shot over them bows is a fight, you mean," said Bob Fea, evidently an argumentative type. "Slavers has lots of men, for to keep the blacks down, but no space for cannon, 'cept on the topdeck. A couple from th' bow-chasers'll do her." The bow wave and spume kept the three of us quite damp; my two companions kept the rest of the sick-bay well informed as to the ships' relative positions. The chase went on and on; finally one of us kept watch out the port while the others sat on the deck.

The sudden boom of the bow-chasers over my head made me jump, prompting chuckles from the sailors. Behind us we heard the gun-trucks rolling out, portside only, because the Revenge didn't have enough healthy men to man both sides of the ship and do sailhandling as well. I could smell the acrid slow-matches from the gundeck. The slaver's name on the stern was now visible— The Black Swan ---.

We had drawn abreast of the slave-ship, a long, low, fast-looking ship quite like the one in Bristol; she did lack a foremast, and was wallowing along slowly compared to us. "Be glad we're upwind, lads!" came from behind us. Another voice said "Pity the prize-crew." I nodded, remembering the stench of the deserted ship at dock in Bristol. The Black Swan's crew were swarming around their deck guns, the tiny tops of their heads appearing periodically.

One more shot across her bows apparently convinced her captain; unable to run away because of the ruined mast, and unable to match weight of metal with the American frigate, sails were loosed and a white flag run up. The Revenge hove to, and above us I could dimly hear the tramping of feet and the rumbling of block and tackle as a large ship's boat was lowered. The American's gun-crews remained at the ready, slow-matches still burning, as the well-armed party, led by Lt McCully, rowed across the heaving sea toward the slaver, the entire ship's boat disappearing periodically in a trough in the waves.

"Listen," said one of the sailors. Over the slap and splash of the sea on the hull, we could hear a lowing, a sort of bleating, coming from the slaver. "Tis the darkies, they never stop until they're on deck," said one of the men. "Don't sound like I remember, though."

"Where is he going?" I whispered, for the ship's boat was rowing around the Black Swan's stern, rather than making for the ladder in plain sight.

"The Lieutenant's a smart one, " said a voice behind. "He's got his reasons." A slaver's officer had appeared at the ladder, waiting for our crew, then disappeared. For a whole minute nothing happened. Then we saw the white smoke from a musket-shot out the slaver's stern-windows; our ship's boat appeared, pulling so hard the bow was almost out of the water, and Lieutenant McCully's sword was flashing up and down, up and down.

"Fire! He's tellin' 'em to broadside her !" shouted Bob Fea, elbowing me out the way. And indeed within two seconds the entire side of our ship exploded and was immediately shrouded in white smoke. A moment later our ship shuddered with the impact of the slaver's cannonballs, followed by the roar of her cannon. The smoke just began to clear a bit and the American guncrews followed almost immediately with a very ragged second broadside, and once again we were blind. I looked behind me at the sick-bay; men were cheering and punching each other, as if there were no butcher's bill for these moments. Dr Monroe, to my amaze, was lying, apparently asleep, on his own operating table.

Then the smoke cleared completely, and we could see the damage wrought to the Black Swan. It appeared a malevolent giant with a hammer had systematically smashed in her whole starboard side. One more broadside from the Revenge, and it was over.

This time, The Black Swan struck her colours in earnest, and Dr Monroe (who really had been asleep, and was not drinking) and I were rowed over to see to the slaver's wounded. She did have a large crew, and all who could stand were herded toward the bow on deck under the bayoneted muskets of the watchful American marines. Dr Monroe and I went below to the slave deck.

I expected rows of miserable humanity, shackled head to foot, in a fetid low warren of despair. What we found was totally unexpected - a gun-deck about the size of the frigate's. No slaves anywhere in sight, just dismounted guns, smashed-out gunports, wood splinters the size of cricket-bats, blood on the deck, cannonballs rolling about, and many dead and wounded. We got to work.

It appeared that the gunports were just a very light wood, laid in and painted to match the hull, with a narrow slit for aiming the cannon. Her captain apparently had planned to fire a broadside at us straight through the wood. Every detail, down to the gun crews moaning like blacks in chains when the Revenge came within ear-shot. No slaver, The Black Swan was a pirate. The American crew, though happy to prevail with so little loss on our side (how quickly they had become 'us' and 'our') were despondent at the loss of a slave cargo and much of their prize-money, their second loss within a week.

Later, the doctor and I stood unsteadily at the slaver's taffrail, taking a moment. Below, rebel Marines had the remaining sound pirates hard at the aft and forward pumps. I looked across at the Revenge, sails furled, heaving gently.

"Murderous dogs— look at that, Hawkins," said Dr Monroe, pointing forward; I spied the foremast, secured to the deck. he said, "They've got a block and tackle rigged. They could ship that mast in under an hour and be under full sail again."

I murmured, "The Black Swan's clipped wing. Clever - lure your prey close and cannon them at point-blank range."

The American Lieutenant McCully emerged from below. One of the Revenge's sailors ask Lieutenant McCully how he had known to give the order to fire.   McCully, his round fair face just as smoke-blown and exhausted as when I first saw him, smiled faintly and looked around the deck, and up in the rigging, and then down at the deck below.   He said,

"It was the smell— she didn't smell at all."

Schooner

Hispaniola

Chapter 8.

The Blackbirder

Connor, the wizened American powder-boy, came running, wide-eyed, apparently up from below. "Lieutenant ! Dr Monroe ! Come below and see this !" Monroe motioned for me to follow him and McCully. It had become dark, and the few lanthorns that could be found were spaced about the gundeck, barely cutting the gloom. The few pirate crew that were still on the pumps looked off nervously, ostentatiously ignoring our group as we followed the youngster. We collected Couevel, pirate first mate, followed by his own Marine, now armed with a dagger and pistol. Down, down we went, below the lower hold, into the very bilges, a very odorous space indeed, so far below the sound of the carpenters' mauls faded away. Crouched, we all followed young Connor forward, sloshing through the foul, ill-smelling black water along the row of ballast-stones to an unexpected bulkhead with a door, making a tiny cabin, far below the water-line.

The first mate drew back, bumping into the rebel Marine behind him. "Kill me—" he muttered. "Kill me, he will, for losing the ship—"

Shaking his head, Lt McCully grabbed a lanthorn, pushed open the cabin door and entered.

"Great God!" he cried, and backed out quickly, breathing heavily. He was pale, and looked around wildly, as if not seeing us. He closed his eyes for a moment, motioned for Dr Monroe to come forward, and re-entered the cabin.

I crowded behind the Doctor; crouched in the doorway, I saw McCully and Monroe bent over a figure lying on the rough decking - a figure whose bare, dirty feet were at least double the size of my own.

"He's alive," said Dr Monroe to the Lieutenant. "Head injury, shallow breathing— we need to get him out of here."

We all exited the cabin. McCully looked at Couevel, and said, "How'd you get him down here?"

The first mate muttered, "Hammocks— eight men."

"Who is he?"

"He the captain - Duco de Rijk."

Lt McCully said to the powder-boy, "Connor, rouse eight men and some hammocks or a small sail. We have to move him out of here."

We had to turn that huge form on its side just to get it through the doorway. It took ten strong men, crouching and shuffling and splashing through the dark, to convey our burden out of the bilges, up to the gundeck and into the captain's cabin, mightily smashed by our round-shot. With the several lanthorns hung near the sleeping-pallet, we got our first really good look at this specimen: long, dirty blond hair, a fearsome bushy beard, and fully seven feet or more long, but built like an outscale blacksmith. His hands were the size of dinner-platters. He looked to be a full head taller than Yellow Jack, and probably weighed twenty-five stone. The cabin was larger than any I had seen; it had an outsize bed, several chairs made to his scale, and headroom. Had it not been filthy as a sty, even before the battle, it could have been charming.

Dr Monroe, bending over Duco de Rijk's head wound, said , "He appears to have been hit by falling tackle or a round-shot. We'll have to wait for daylight; though why I should extend myself to save this creature, who will need a special gallows, is beyond me." The doctor sent me back to check on the status of the pirates in sick-bay, with permission to sleep if I could. I could.

In the morning, both ships were under sail and were wallowing along south and west at two or three knots while repairs continued. Whilst we were working on the pirate captain's depressed head-fracture, Dr Monroe said, "Hawkins, Captain Conyngham came across to the Black Swan during the night. He made a cursory inspection, and issued orders to Lt McCully and myself. This morning I am to return to the Revenge. The Lieutenant is taking this ship as a prize and is to make sail for the nearest friendly port. You and the crew from the Hispaniola will stay aboard, to be paroled ashore. You are temporarily this ship's medicoe."

Surprised, I exclaimed, "We are not Royal Navy, that anyone will be exchanging prisoners for us, Doctor. And what about this head-wound? And the other wounded?"

The Doctor nodded wearily. "I am sorry, Hawkins, it is either go with this ship and at least step ashore, or travel with the Revenge indefinitely in war-time. As for the giant, I can do nothing. He is in a coma, from which he will emerge, or not, as Providence deems fit. Keep him well watered. That man is a lusus naturae, a freak of nature. I have never seen a larger man. Beware, if he should ever get loose. For the others, you can keep them as healthy as I; the ones which are to live, will live." Dr Monroe had become something of a philosopher in the past 24 hours.

As the Black Swan had no sort of dispensary, I prevailed upon Dr Monroe to allow me to accompany him back to the Revenge. While laying in a small stock of medical supplies, I also managed to obtain and conceal Flint's treasure-map. And then back to the Black Swan.

The remaining Hispaniolas had all been brought over, and they cried greetings and all thumped me on the back, and looked around the ship, in the moments before they were whisked away to set sail. Captain Conyngham, already short-handed, had only given McCully six Marines and ten seamen from the Revenge.

Thus it was that the Revenge and Black Swan parted ways, just at noon. I watched as the Revenge sailed away north, until only the white of her upper yards could be seen.

All hands were called, and Lt McCully spoke to us from the quarterdeck, saying the Black Swan was a prize to the American Navy, that the pirates were going to prison or be hanged, and said the Hispaniolas would work watch and watch with the American sailors, and in return we would be dropped at the nearest South American port and given our freedom.

"A Spanish port without doubt," called Sam Dresser. "No British trade, 'cause of the war, and us'll die of the Yellow Jack afore we see England again. ----- your Freedom," and he spat on the deck.

McCully stared at Dresser for a moment and said in a stronger voice, "Hispaniolas, our countries are at war and I am within my rights to press any of you. Do not abuse my liberality."

He began to turn away when Jan, one of our remaining Dutchmen, said slowly, in the longest speech I had heard him make, at least in English, "Kapitien, we are told that Holland has entered this war on the side of the American Colonies. Is this true? If so, we Nederlanders are your allies and you have no right to abandon us in Spanish America."

McCully nodded slowly. "You're correct. However - this is not a passenger vessel. I am authorized to accept you Dutchmen as enlisting in the Navy of the United States." I did not imagine that the Dutch were eager for combat. McCully turned and spoke quietly to the Marine sergeant. The conversation seemed to be over.

I went below to the improvised sick-berth and attended to the men. Some light and air was coming down through the hatches. The pirate crew in sickbay were a mixed, murderous, sullen lot, some Swedes, some Germans, several Portugees, a Spaniard or two, and several mute Indians. I was cleaning the ploughed-up thigh of one Paulo, 'from Napoli', a vicious little knife-fighter if ever I saw one, and asked, "Tell me about the Captain."

"They call him The Giant."

"Where is he from? What is his story?"

Paulo squinted for a moment. "He speak some Dutch, mos'ly English. Cap'n Duco was a famous strong man in Europe— kill a man, run to sea. I been with him three year."

From behind us, a grizzled pirate with a mass of nasty slashes laughed and coughed at once, and said, "That ain't all he's killed, mate. Duco ain't a Dutchman - he's from Cardiff. Weren't twenty, I heard he killed three men in a tavern, stole a boat for Amsterdam and never went back, took a Dutch name, worked in a circus all over Europe." It made sense to me— Duco could hardly blend in anywhere, and if he was a known murderer in both Britain and the Continent, then the sea was his only escape, and piracy his only possible pursuit.

Turning to the elder pirate, a Briton, I said, "Tell me your name."

"Grimwood, young sir."

"Where are you from?"

A tiny half-smile appeared amid the stubble. "Me'en a Cornish wrecker, young sir. Me Da and his Da before him. Wreck 'em and scrag the crew, we did. "

"Tell me about this ship."

He shifted uncomfortably in his hammock. "Ay, there's a tale. We had a tiny schooner, hove to, yards slack, ye ken? Us seen this slaver, he came near, her captain boarded us, and Duco carried him abovedeck, said he'd strangle the fellow 'less we could come on board. We boarded and carried her, crew overboard, sold the slaves, them as lived, anyroad."

"And whose idea was remodelling the slave deck into a gundeck?"

Paulo broke in. "Cap'n Duco make us spend four months, Signore, working on this b_____d. Even made us change the ballast. Then we didn't have no guns."

"Slaver's a rich prize, mate," said the elder pirate. "Duco played the same game as with the schooner, and we got a fourth-rate wi' eighteen-pounders, Royal Navy, she was."

"We never heard of losing a Royal Navy ship to a Duco the Pirate in these waters," I said.

"Poor lads, all lost in a storm at sea, they was - sunk in a thousand fathoms." Grimwood positively leered at this.

Paulo laughed, "Dead men don't bite, you know!"

Grimwood said, "Strange thing, though - Duco was freebooting for mebbe ten years before I joined him - same time as you" (this last to Paulo) "..where's his old ship? His crew? You ever meet one of his earlier crew?" Paulo shook his head. Grimwood's voice rose. "Where's his treasure, matey?"

Duco's was a most malevolent intelligence, I mused, able to modify a slaver into a formidable disguised vessel, fox the British Navy and take a fourth-rate by treachery, gaining its guns; witty enough to create a pun with the ship's name - the Black Swan, blackbirder. Some time later I heard a clanking and clunking and muttered oaths, and turned to see six sweating, gasping Marines carrying the chain-wrapped unconscious body of Duco the Giant, followed by Acting Captain McCully. The Marines dumped Duco unceremoniously on a pallet made of sailcloth. I was white with anger, and stared at Lt McCully with clenched fists.

"Medicoe," said McCully, "What was your name?"

"Hawkins. And it is a most un-Christian thing you do, sir. That man is insensible, and may not live."

"Well, Hawkins, I need the main cabin, and he belongs in sick-bay. Will he die soon?" he asked, looking out the companion-way, not meeting my eyes, I thought.

"Dr Monroe suspects he has the head-fracture, sir, and he said it could go either way. No, he is breathing strongly, I doubt he die this day."

"A pity." And Lieutenant Thomas McCully walked away, head down, mulling, followed by the Marines.

Several hours passed. I liberally dosed those in pain with alcoholic tincture of opium. I asked a few more questions about Duco and the history of this ship, but Duco's presence stifled any replies. I gave Duco some water, which he reflexively swallowed. He was snoring loudly, on his back, with chains at his hands and feet. I estimated he was fully seven feet tall, or, rather long, lying there. I was just back from emptying some pans when I heard the jingling of Marines, and there was McCully again, followed by the apparently inevitable crowd of Marines.

"We have come for the prisoner, Medicoe." Turning to a Marine, he said, "Chains off, rope his hands."

"Captain, that man is unconscious - what do you intend?"

"My duty." McCully's round face was unnatural, set, and he waited until the Marines removed the chains and wrapped a hempen rope around Duco's wrists. "To the deck, men."

Around me, wounded pirates had risen in their hammocks, a babble of tongues protesting. I left them and hurried up on deck.

It was a beautiful late afternoon; the Black Swan was heeled over slightly in the breeze, most of the undamaged sails set and drawing deeply. The foremast was still down and there was still rigging dangling over the sides; the ship was far from 'shipshape and Bristol fashion'. Lt McCully stood alone on the quarterdeck, back toward us, looking out at our wake.

Allan and Yellow Jack motioned me over. Allan whispered sotto voce, "Mr Jim, we hear they're hangin' the Giant, him bein' still out of his senses!" I nodded, looking around at the preparations in disbelief. The American sailors had run a line up to a pulley on the end of the mainmast crosstree. One of them had already fashioned a hangman's knot. The Giant lay on his side on the deck while they fitted the noose, looking like children at play in comparison to his great size. All the Marines and several of the sailors had the other end of the line.

I turned to Allan and Yellow Jack. "That's it? They're simply going to strangle him slowly?"

Jack leaned down and whispered. "Aye, no trap door o'mercy to fall and break HIS neck - aye, he'll die soon enough. He'd have had our hearts, every one, make no mistake."

McCully, alone on the quarterdeck, slowly turned around and looked down at us all. He called out in that flat, nasal voice, "Sergeant, do your duty."

The Marine sergeant nodded to the men on the line, and they began backing away, just as if they were loading heavy goods out of the hold. The rope tightened, and Duco's head and neck lifted. The crew kept pulling, and in a moment his feet were off the deck, rising slowly, almost over the lee rail. His body kept rising until his feet were about twenty feet off the deck, and the crew secured the line. The noose had cut cruelly into his neck, his face red with trapped blood., body twisting in the wind.

To my shock, I saw Duco's feet begin to kick - his eyes were open and looking around. Jack's great hand was gripping my shoulder tightly. My mind was racing— it was theoretically possible for a person with head fracture to become conscious because of additional trauma, but I had never imagined such a thing. Duco was definitely conscious, and the American crew were murmuring and pointing. Kicking his feet wildly, Duco flexed and strained his arms, and stretched the rope around his wrists until it loosened, and he flung it away. I had never seen such strength, in a blacksmith nor a professional strongman. His hands free, he reached above his head and grasped the line, taking the strain off his neck. Holding on with one hand, the other hand clawed at the noose. I could clearly hear his first great gasping gulp of breath. Looking up, Duco began swarming up the line, pulling his great weight straight up by the power in his arms alone, until he hooked his leg over the crosstree, and then was seated, removing the noose. He dropped the line and looked down at us on the the deck for the first time, panting, his hair and beard blowing wildly with the breeze, the crosstree end swaying out over the water with every plunge of the ship.

McCully suddenly ran down the quarterdeck stairs, heading for the muskets, stacked far forward, bawling, "Sergeant! Shoot him!" The Marines looked about confusedly, unsure what to do.

Duco suddenly jumped off the crosstree, his huge body in midair forever, then plunged into the sea, out of sight.

The entire crew rushed to the side - he was gone.

Schooner

Hispaniola

Part III. - THE HISPANIOLA

Chapter 9.

Narrative Continued By Doctor Livesey:

Voyage To Treasure Island

Voyage Day 11, David Livesey's Journal: aboard Hispaniola

With anguish in my heart, I watched the Americans hastily row back to their ship and make sail, without so much as a jeering thanks for the crew. We could all see the billowing white sails of a square-rigged Royal Navy three-decker, still hull-down, but growing quickly.

Captain Conyngham and his Lieutenant had been extremely suspicious of the story we told; our hold, empty of trade goods, gave us the lie. Kapitein von Loendersloot had resorted to speaking and understanding no English at all; all discourse with the Americans was done laboriously through his bosun van der Heijden, with many deliberate mistakes in translation and requests for repetition, to where they angrily left him alone. Conyngham had the cabin area searched thoroughly. Twice. If the treasure map had been found we would have all been in a tight spot. As it was, every man Jack of our crew knew Hispaniola was on a treasure-voyage, and Jim was there with them, pressed onto the American frigate, with the map on his person. I had not thought that through sufficiently well, I am afraid.

There were eight of us left standing on the main deck, Trelawney and myself, the Kapitein, the coxswain, Laemmers the first mate, van der Heijden the bosun, Klagg the bosun's mate, and the second mate, all watching the two other ships, in a frozen tableau: 'Midmorning, Hispaniola Schooner, Somewhere in the West Indies'. Soon the Revenge was hull-down near the horizon, having fled due south. Of course, from the deck of the Hispaniola, the horizon was only 6 miles away.

The Royal Navy seventy-four was upon us, losing way as she passed on our starboard side, enormous, three times our length, looking like a city block afloat. Across the water came a faint bellow. "Sir! His Majesty's Ship Percheron— do you require assistance?"

The Kapitein roared, "NO!" and the seventy-four gun ship raised all sail, following the American toward the horizon. The Hispaniola was rolling considerably in the morning sunlight, with no way on her, most sails furled hastily.

"Now, Livesey," said von Loendersloot, "no more 'just sail southwest by south, there's a good fellow' - the map and the exact bearings of the island I must have."

"Just one moment, Kapitein," blustered Trelawney, "we just lost our entire crew, I say— this ship should repair to the nearest friendly port."

The Kapitein sneered, "Nearest is up the Bristol Channel, Trelawney. England is with every nation in this hemisphere at war."

Laemmers, the first mate, had emerged from the cabin with a roll of charts, seated himself on the deck, and unrolled a large one showing the northeast shoulder of the South American continent; dotted here and there along a semicircle were the various islands of the West Indies. Laemmers peered at the map closely, traced his way with one grimy forefinger to a spot a handsbreadth northeast of the rightmost curve of islands, and muttered in Dutch, "We are here, Mynheer Kapitein."

Von Loendersloot gave it a glance and turned to me again. "Doctor, you the owner are, but I am the Kapitein. The creditors, if we return with nothing, will ruin Trelawney, I am certain. I again ask, where is the map of Flint, and what are the bearings to the island!" His face was dangerously red.

"I no longer have the map, Kapitein."

He shook his head slowly. "No tricks - do you prize the life of this man?" The Kapitein had moved next to Trelawney and from somewhere in that black cloak of his, produced a small flintlock pistol, and thrust it against the Squire's belly. "You are a doctor - you know the death he will have if I here shoot. Now give the map!"

Trelawney's blue eyes were very wide indeed, watching me, the Kapitein, and especially that squat, ugly little pistol in von Loendersloot's fist. I kept my voice level. "We need to head for the Leeward Isles. The bearings of the island are 18 degrees 4 minutes North, 64 degrees 21 minutes West."

Laemmers scrawled them in pencil on the chart, one day east and slightly south of Ponce on Porto Rico isle. He looked up at the Kapitein and told him, again in Dutch, that it was four days' sail, if the weather held.

Von Loendersloot's granite face had not changed nor relaxed. "Where is the map to the island, Livesey?"

"I tell you, we don't have it - I gave it to one of the crew for safekeeping, and now they are all pressed by the Americans."

"Which one?"

"No matter - the map was superfluous." Seeing his puzzlement, I continued hastily, "The markings on the map were not useful anyway. The bar silver was moved and reburied before our arrival in the year sixty-five."

"Moved by who?"

"A maroon named Ben Gunn found all the treasure, and moved all excepting the bar silver to a cave."

"So where is the bar silver, and how do you know what is there?"

By this time Trelawney had regained some of his bluster. "Seven hundred thousand pound, Kapitein, and none save Livesey and myself know where it lies.. so none of your fuss, and put that away, I say -" He pushed the pistol away, and to my surprise the Kapitien acquiesced.

He looked at his officers, everyone totally done in from the long night's chase. We all had been awake for well over twenty-four hours. The Kapitein closed his eyes. "Food we must have, and rest." He started for the cabin.

I tried one more time. "Surely there are ports where we could pick up some hands."

Turning back to me, the Kapitein said, "Doctor, this is a small schooner. Sail we could with three seamen. We will go to the island directly. No need for provisions, no need for more crew - no reasons at all to take time in port, perhaps a pirate crew we get. No - you and the fat man will work!"

Voyage Day 12, David Livesey's Journal: aboard Hispaniola

The next morning Trelawney and I were roused early by the coxswain. I entered the main cabin and determined that the glass was falling, meaning weather was coming, and then I crept sleepily out onto the wet, slightly-canted deck.   The day was grey and it had been raining lightly. Laemmers, the first mate, and the bosun, Loes van der Heijden, sat gloomily on the deck, sorting out a damp mass of cordage, block and tackle.   I looked up, and the Hispaniola was skating along minus its topsails, and of the foresails, only the flying jib was rigged. Klagg was at the tiller. The course was WSW toward the island. We were sailing a broad reach, across the Southeast trades, and the men barely had to touch a sail hours on end.   It was wonderful sailing, only tempered by the fact that it was nearly hurricane season - and that the glass was falling.

"Gentlemen," the Kapitein greeted us almost cheerily. "We save you climbing -" he gestured at the tackle on deck - "raise, lower foresail, mainsail, less work for all."

Laemmers muttered in Dutch to no one in particular that we should worry about winning the anchor, not a bit of climbing. Still concealing my understanding, I reflected to myself that was true, that it normally took ten to fifteen hands' heavy work on the foc'sle deck to weigh the anchor.

The Kapitien shook his head at Laemmers, turned to the Squire and myself. "I am hungry. Your assignment is to make for the crew breakfast. And soon, Doctor, you will make a new map for us."

Trelawney muttered to himself all the way belowdecks.

Voyage Day 13, David Livesey's Journal: aboard Hispaniola

On this day, seated in the main cabin, I drew a rough picture of the island for von Loendersloot. I drew the outline, roughly the shape of a lumpy potato stood on end, and some of the features, minus of course the actual location of the bar silver that Ben had reburied. When I was finished I called the Kapitein in, along with Laemmers, and together we examined my drawing.

"There are three main hills, north to south," I said, pointing, "the northernmost is called Foremast Hill, the highest one in the middle is called Spyglass Hill, because you can see twenty miles to the horizon in every direction, and down south next to Capt. Kidd's anchorage, that is called Mizzenmast Hill."

"Where is this cave of Ben Gunn?" asked the Kapitein.

"Here." I pointed at a twin-peaked hill midway between Spyglass and Foremast hills. "It is about one mile to the North Inlet."

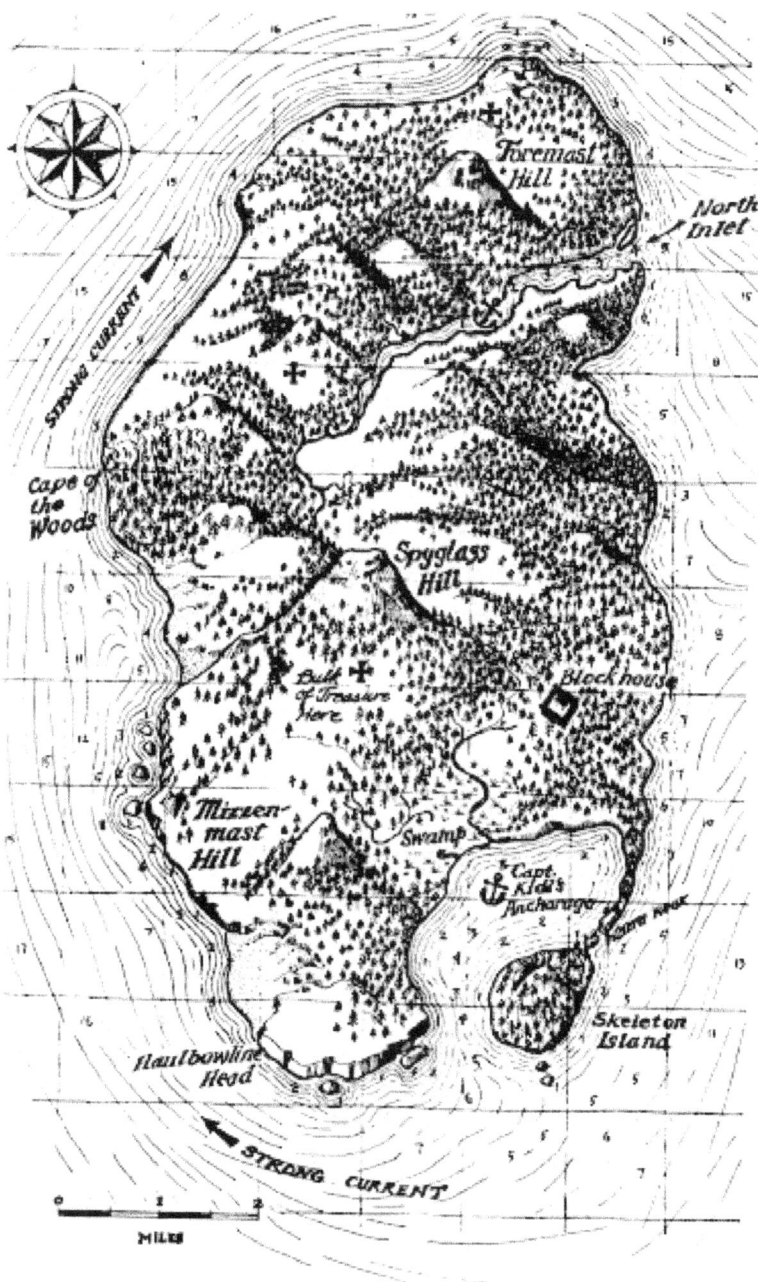

This map is rumoured to have been drawn by RL Stevenson.

"Southeast tradewind is now strong, almost hurricane season." Von Loendersloot pointed at Capt. Kidd's anchorage. "This bay on the south end, it is no good, trades blowing on a lee shore, can enter with no problem. Leaving, we must warp or tow ship out to the entrance, need bigger crew, and still is a chance of here grounding -" and he pointed at the steep cliffs and at the rocks off the aptly named Haulbowline Head. He went on, "Current will be clockwise around this island, strong north current on west side, coming around the north end." Von Loendersloot continued to focus on the map. "This North Inlet - what depth?"

I said, "Four fathoms to here, where we anchored. It has a very small entrance, east and west. It's one more mile by water to the trail to the cave - all together, one mile of rowing, one mile of climbing."

With his finger firmly on the North Inlet, he said, "Good. Here we will anchor."

Later that day we passed north of Barbuda, only dimly visible through the rain, and at dusk, in the face of a heavy sea and rain, passed south of St. Barthelemy, although we could not see it at all.

Voyage Day 14, David Livesey's Journal: aboard Hispaniola

Continued voyage toward island. Rain continued, dripping into the cabins from all the seams in the deck. Other than hauling on an occasional line, Trelawney's and my duty was limited to functioning as the ship's cooks; it was extremely strange to work in the galley where that infamous villain Silver once jigged around on his wooden crutch; indeed, the decking in the galley was much pockmarked. There in the corner was the perch where his parrot once shrieked. That parrot's foul and violent language alone should have been sufficient to alert both Trelawney and me to its owner's true character; but the wretch was so good at dissembling he fooled everyone, child and adult, save Capt Smollett, bless his suspicious heart.

Chapter 10.

Narrative Continued By The Doctor :

End Of The Hispaniola ; Marooned

Voyage Day 15, David Livesey's Journal: aboard Hispaniola

Other than the weather steadily worsening, slowing us by variable winds, the days had passed uneventfully, if always-wet clothing and being continually called on deck to haul on lines could be called uneventful.   Trelawney was much better, to my surprise; he seemed to revel in the weather, his cheeks ruddy and his blue eyes sparkling, seemingly forgetful that we had lost control of the voyage and of our ship; von Loendersloot was clearly, at least to me, merely enduring our presence until the bar silver was in hand.   Subsequently, whether our charade of owner and captain would be preserved, I had no guesses.

The wind picked up force mid-morning, the Hispaniola's stem plunging deep, wild random waves all around. Sail was reduced to a scrap to maintain her heading WSW and a quarter south. Holding on to the quarterdeck ladder on my way into the main cabin, I made no mistake, it was getting serious, and we were nearing the island, according to the Kapitein.

"I have planned poorly, Livesey," he said, staring at his charts. He had been on deck much in the past days, and his grizzled cheeks and sunken eyes made him look like a very sunburned cadaver in a black cloak. "We should have hove to near Barbuda. This is not good. We have St. Christoph, you call St. Kitt, already passed."

I had nothing to offer. It was unusual for him to share his thoughts on any subject whatsoever; perhaps an emergency called to one's common humanity.

"The sun has been, how you say, hiding, and we have no good noon reading for days," said the Kapitein, "but van der Heijden believes us to be only hours from your island. We will pass very near, and will tack back when this weather vollendet ist." He must have been tired, to lapse into Dutch with me.

His plan, however sound, was not meant to be. It was all hands for hours. Sometime in the midafternoon, Hispaniola plunging like an unbroken horse on the starboard tack, all of us suddenly heard the boom of surf dead ahead. Through the rain we could see the dim outline of hills, much too close. The Kapitein immediately shoved the tiller over, trying to bear off to port. The island promptly disappeared in the rain. It had to be ours— there were no other islands on the chart. Of course, our island was not on the chart. Shouting in Dutch, von Loendersloot managed to head us straight south, I assumed, as we heard the breakers booming off to our right. When the booming stopped, I assumed we were clear of the island, but the Kapitein changed her heading to due west in the heavy rain, with the island to the north of us, and I realised he was trying to circle the island, get off this lee shore, and find the North Inlet anchorage.

The current that sweeps clockwise around the island had us; I could feel the extra speed. The Kapitein took in more sail. Though we were still blind, we were on the windward side of the island, heading north - the wind was on our nose; von Loendersloot called to the bosun on the foc'sle deck, telling him to take heed. Unneeded, Trelawney and I crept forward to see better, and suddenly, on the starboard bow, out of the rain and fog, loomed the island. Von Loendersloot wrestled with the tiller, trying to bear port, but the current ignored both the wind and the rudder. The deck was canted and Trelawney were looking at each other in horror at the moment the Hispaniola struck.

The ship had been moving at seven or eight knots and stopped instantly; Trelawney and I were off our feet, though we both held onto the lines strung about the deck. I could see the boom break loose, almost braining von Loendersloot. Then the masts fell forward with a horrible cracking sound, and I realised that my beautiful schooner was breaking up. She was down by the stem, and the stern was rising, being pushed by the current.

One more wrenching slew sideways, and Trelawney and I were in the water.

Voyage Day 16, David Livesey's Journal: On the Island
The poor Hispaniola had smashed onto the rocks offshore of Mizzenmast Hill. Trelawney and I were swept northward by the current and, swimming frantically towards the shore on our right, we were finally dumped by the heavy surf onto a small beach to the north. I struggled to my feet and peered through the rain and fog, and thought I saw two heads in the surf. I shouted to them and indeed Jos von Loendersloot and Jan Laemmers

the first mate navigated the surf and were soon on the beach. Trelawney had swallowed seawater, and for about an hour he and von Loendersloot were weakly sick. Sitting on the sand in the cool rain, we did not know if the others had survived or were drowned.   I thought I knew where we were; an inland march and climb to the northeast would, I opined, lead us to Ben Gunn's cave, with its blessed freshwater spring, where I hoped and prayed we might find a discarded flint and steel.

Voyage Day 17, David Livesey's Journal: On the Island

Food was a serious problem.   While none had espied any of the goat population, it was a moot point because we had no usable firearms, powder, or shot.   Trelawney and von Loendersloot were feeling much better.   We did, at least, have fresh water and the means to make a fire.   This day the two Dutch were planning to swim out to the wreck of my poor Hispaniola, hoping to dive into her hold, attempting to find enough tools aboard to make a raft or small boat.   This was wise - unless we found sustenance soon, we would become too weak for such feats of athleticism.   Von Loendersloot was of two minds, though — he also wished to find and excavate the silver cache.

Thus in the morning Trelawney and I made the easy descent from the cave to the head of the North Inlet, where we had hoped to anchor.   We found sea-urchin, crab, and clams, and returned to the cave.   Back in sixty-five we had left a pewter pot in the cave, and thus we began a savoury seafood soup which proved popular later when the Kapitein and Laemmers returned, triumphantly holding a shovel, an adze, a musket, shot and soaked powder, all retrieved from the cabin and hold.   Soaked and chilled, they sipped their soup using shells as spoons.   The Kapitein reported there was no sight of Loes van der Heijden the bosun, Klagg or the coxswain or of the second mate. He also said the Hispaniola was badly broken up on the rocks and would never sail again. I nursed my hot soup and mourned.

Voyage Day 18, David Livesey's Journal: On the Island

In the afternoon, earlier having spread the gunpowder to dry, having gathered clams and mussels, and having started more soup, I was atop Spyglass Hill, scanning the horizon for anything other than poor weather. One aspect of being marooned on a tropical isle is that it affords ample time for reflection. Where was Jim? Where was the crew? Were they alive? I could not see the Americans harming them - perhaps pressed as crew, perhaps traded in Spanish America. The reluctant Doctor James Hawkins: entirely too ready with his fists, genuinely intelligent, superficially cultured, somewhat travelled, somewhat prosperous, definitely ambitious.

This last recalled to me the day of his arrival in Bristol. Fresh off the coach, Jim accosted me in my rooms in the Old Anchor Inn, giving me the benefit of his thoughts of Trelawney. "He is an old fool," Jim hissed to me. "He has managed to LOSE twenty times MY net worth !" The Oxford coach would try the patience of a saint.

A thought occurred which might explain this heat: "James, do you have racing-debt you cannot meet?"

"No, I do not, and if I did, that is not germane to the advantage taken of me when I was a child. Ten out of three hundred fifty thousand!"

That old grievance again. Mrs Hawkins had been frantic for weeks, not knowing if her boy was lost. Her joy and gratitude upon his safe return to England was overwhelming. It took more than a month for Trelawney's bank to serve up an accounting of the treasure. When we sat down for a reckoning with Mrs Hawkins and Jim, it was difficult to prevail upon her to accept even ten thousand pound - such an unimaginable sum to them then. Of course Jim would not remember it as I did. I spoke: "Perhaps this new voyage is our opportunity to redress any inequities, and to fill the coffers, as it were."

His face was white and he seemed angry. "If I had not handed the map to you two, you would have gained nothing... and to casually toss a tiny fraction of the whole to the person, albeit a young boy, that had created the opportunity is... unethical."

"Possibly," I replied, "but less ethical men would have taken the map, patted you on the head, said, 'We'll look into this, my boy,' and sent you on your way, no voyage, no ten thousand pounds."

He softened. "Ah, that could not have happened. You were there, Doctor."

Nonetheless, Jim drove a hard bargain. When we later joined the Squire, Jim went on the offensive. "Very well, gentlemen, you wish my attendance upon this voyage, as a spy. What is your proposal?"

I feared I had the drift already. Trelawney looked puzzled. "Proposal? We propose you assist in securing the remainder of the treasure, Hawkins," said the Squire, looking round at me in his vague way. "I thought this was all agreed upon."

Jim pounced on these last words. "That is an excellent thought, Squire - we require an agreement, a legal agreement between gentlemen," he said quickly and impatiently, "one which clearly spells out in advance of the voyage the subsequent division of any spoils; further, it should include rights of survivorship."

"I say, that's rather abrupt," spluttered Trelawney, "and smacks of lack of trust. I am dismayed."

Before Jim could utter what was clearly on his lips, I said, "Perhaps it would be best, as we are all risking our lives, when only one of us is in current jeopardy." The Squire's big blue eyes looked reproachfully at me.

In time, the following agreement was hammered out:

> 200,000 pounds to Trelawney's creditors. Of the remainder,
> 40% to Livesey (200,000 pounds)
> 40% to Hawkins (200,000 pounds)
> 20% to Trelawney (100,000 pounds)

This last after much squawking and harrumphing from the Squire. Jim's inflexible position was that we, besides risking our lives, were granting him sufficient to permanently mollify his creditors; Jim also made the point that, assuming the silver was worth seven hundred thousand, the Squire would in effect have taken three hundred thousand of the whole, compared to our two hundred apiece. The agreement being duly signed by all, Jim carried the day.

Of course, I thought, sitting on my rock, looking out at the great circle of empty sea, that is all by the wayside; can't eat silver - crew pressed and gone, Hispaniola lost; we were, theoretically, the richest maroons in the world.

Voyage Day 19, David Livesey's Journal: On the Island
As our tools now included a shovel, the Kapitein was with child to excavate the silver. Trelawney wished to stay behind in the cave and tend the stew; thus it was that an eager von Loendersloot and an indifferent Laemmers

accompanied me around the shoulder of Ben's hill, northeast toward Foremast Hill and the spot to where a superstitious Ben Gunn had laboriously carried and re-buried Flint's silver ingots. In the year sixty-five I had indeed done a bit of surveying of this cache and had reburied it, as our party had been eager to make sail for England.

Now I am not one given much to hyperbole; but I give my affdavy, as the sailors say, that on this occasion von Loendersloot would have killed me on the spot with his nasty little pistol, if he could. For the silver was not there. Like the mutineers all those years ago, we were standing before an excavated crater, well-weathered, not recent. The Kapitein leaped in and started madly kicking the sides of the hole: a remarkable exhibition in one normally so self-contained. "Wo ist es ?!?" he screamed at the heavens. I did not know, but I had the glimmer of an idea.

Laemmers saw it just as I did, a corner of a stained chest amongst the mud. He pointed at it, and the Kapitein was scrabbling at it with his fingers. The first mate jumped into the hole with the shovel, and between them they soon uncovered a long greenstained brassbound leather and wooden chest. Laemmers struck off its lock with the shovel, and they eagerly threw back the lid to uncover a bundle wrapped in oiled sailcloth. With his dirk the Kapitein slit the layers to reveal about forty well-preserved, very oily muskets of French manufacture, in a style dating from the 1740's. Booty from some long-sunk victim of Flint's, without a doubt. The presence of the muskets was news to me, and I said so. It is possible these had been untouched since Ben moved them, our party in sixty-five having had no interest in buried firearms.

The Kapitein just stood staring at the muskets. Laemmers methodically stabbed at the earth around the sides of the hole with his shovel, and was soon rewarded with another woody clunk. This chest had a small cache of pistols, with a remarkable bag of roundshot for the muskets, along with two small kegs marked, in French, gunpowder— probably caked and unusable.

Von Loendersloot clambered out of the excavation and stood staring at me. "This is what we have come for, herr Doctor? Where is the verdammte silber, eh?"

I reminded them both that in sixty-five we had left three of Silver's mutineers on the island, and at that time the silver in this hole had only recently been re-buried by myself and Gray, Trelawney's man. I opined that the three maroons had excavated it and probably built a raft and left the island. I also said something about treasure-quests not being a sure thing. It was at that point wet powder saved my life.

There was nothing more to say. Each burdened with several muskets, the shot and a keg of powder, we retraced our steps toward the cave.

Voyage Day 20, David Livesey's Journal: On the Island

The silent, resentful group parted first thing in the morning, the Kapitein and Laemmers headed out with the muskets to try to shoot some goats. My job as cook extended to foraging. I carried several bags with me, and I spent time beneath the dripping forest canopy seeking the nutritious mushroom. No matter where on the island I wandered, the distant thud and boom of the surf was always audible. Around the shoulder of a small hill I came upon an overhang, almost a cave; I could see where someone, Ben Gunn or the maroons, had tried to scrabble some sort of shelter into the side of the hill. It was damp and dark, and with no surprise I found a miniature forest of mushrooms. I stooped and picked one, then turned to the light and examined it. .

My mind cast back to rusty, wizened little Entwistle, fresh back from his own encounter with Capt. Gustavus Conyngham, trying to reach the back gallery of the Royal Society with his reedy voice; he described ritual use of the fungus among the natives of New Spain, and he then described an encounter with some indigenous tribe at inordinate length. While his specimens were so dried as to be unrecognisable, Entwistle was always a good draftsman, and his pen-and-ink drawing of amanita muscaria, Flesh Of The Gods, was remarkably true to life. Regretfully I folded my bag closed and moved on; this was clearly no part of dinner.

The rain had abated, though the air was still damp; our gunpowder would not be dry for some time. I recalled the island did have some few wild vegetables and a small stand of breadfruit trees down in Silver's swamp next to what the mutineers had called Capt. Kidd's anchorage.

I came down from the shoulder of the Mizzenmast, the southernmost hill on the island, into the back of the swamp, looking for breadfruit. I stopped in my tracks, for I heard a regular, distinctly metallic clank coming from my left. I crept quietly, finally wading, as I neared the mouth of the small freshwater stream which bordered and fed the swamp. There, at anchor in the small harbour, was a small, broad-beamed three masted Spanish vessel, sails mostly in tatters, eight portholes visible. There were work crews aloft working on the rigging, and there was a party on the beach, having set up a small forge; thus the hammering I had heard. There was a jolly-boat staked to the beach, with watering casks, riding high, so watering had not been completed. It appeared to be a military vessel of some sort. I laid in the bulrushes and attempted a count; I saw between fifty and sixty men, few armed. I saw a file of men coming from a trail I knew led upwards to Flint's blockhouse. The ship apparently had arrived late the previous day. I crept backward stealthily until I could trot back to the cave to inform Trelawney and the Dutchmen.

On a piece of land of fifty square miles, much of it steep, hilly and heavily wooded, one might expect to elude even a superior force for quite some time. However, I had reckoned without hunting parties. When I arrived at the cave, Trelawney, Kapitein Jos von Loendersloot and Jan Laemmers were already prisoners; when the Spaniards espied me they clapped a pistol to Trelawney's head, waving me to come forward.They were an officer, six armed sailors, and two dead goats. They looked around the cave curiously, took our muskets and goat, and led the four of us, not even deigning to tie our hands, toward their camp at Capt. Kidd's Anchorage.

Part IV

Chapter 11

Narrative continued by James Hawkins

Aboard The Black Swan -- Changing Of The Guard

I am always amazed at how shipboard life parallels that of
a village; no matter what the event, it is known throughout
the community as if there were town criers on every deck,
especially if it was sensational.   Duco's suicidal jump
into the sea had shaken the pirates, the entire American
crew as well as most of the Hispaniolas. Thus the pirates,
both in sickbay and locked below in the hold, knew every
detail. The very idea of hanging an unconscious man was
abhorrent enough: to have a man this feared revive in the
hangman's very noose, escape, yet choose to die, sent a
wave of superstition through the ship.

Some of the pirates in sickbay said that Duco would be
back, spirit or no. They peppered me with questions - had
Duco said anything, did he seem angry, what did he do
while falling into the sea...

"He walk these decks again as uno Spettro, una Fantasma," moaned Paulo. Another, a Spaniard, nodded vigorously and crossed himself muttering about "Duco el Duende."

"Belay that, mate. Duco's only a man, and he's gone, and we're headed for prison or the gallows ourself-moan about that, " growled Grimwood.

In truth, several of these fellows were well enough to be discharged from the sickbay, but I knew the conditions in the hold, hard enough for the healthier pirates. The Americans were headed for the Port of Spain, on the Trinidad island, only a few days' sailing. After a welcome meal, the denizens of sickbay settled in for the night, and I swung in a hammock with the rest.

Our rest only lasted a couple of hours. I was awakened suddenly by a hubbub astern, near the hatches for the hold. It sounded as if the pirates were breaking out. My heart started thumping. The lanthorns had dimmed down and some were out, so we were mostly in the dark, sitting in our swaying hammocks. Something was definitely happening; I heard bare feet running overhead, muffled oaths, steel on steel, muffled cries.

Grimwood writhed out of his hammock. "'Tis Duco, takin' the ship back, mates!" Before any of us could act, lanthorn-light preceded a motley group of heavily-armed, lately-imprisoned pirates, among the swaying hammocks in sickbay. One, an evil-looking palefaced creature with a foot-long dirk in his hand, called to my patients, "Any Americans here?"

Several fingers pointed my way. I was half-in and half out of my hammock. Grimwood spoke up. "Belay, mates, Hawkins here is a Hispaniola - they was McCully's prisoners afore they come aboard. Good sawbones, too."

The pale one said, "No matter-he's in the hold until morning." And they frog-marched me aft, where several lanthorns dimly lit a large pile of clothes and personal effects, and familiar white faces looked up from the blackness of the hold. The hatch cover was nearby, partially smashed or pulled apart. Paleface said to me, "Strip, all but your small-clothes." Since I'd come aboard the Black Swan only two days before, I had the sailcloth packet between my belt and the small of my back. However, several sabres and Paleface's dirk convinced me to divest myself of my clothes, while endeavouring to conceal the packet in my shirt and vest. One of the pirates heard the small clunk as it hit the deck, and he kicked it toward Paleface, who gestured, "Down and in, mate." I sat on the edge of the opening and dropped down, and several hands steadied me as I landed.

I was apparently the last of the newcomers to the hold. A babble of voices in the dark greeted me; through it cut Dutch Jan's tenor voice calling, "Mr Jim! Here!" As I made my way toward his voice through the small crowd of Americans and Hispaniolas, one lanthorn was lowered, and then the hatch was dragged closed.

Jan grasped my arm. He was crouched on the deck, over someone's body. Connor the powder-boy said, "Medicoe, it's the Lieutenant - he's cut up awful." I was surprised that McCully was still alive, I had expected him to be murdered out of hand. I called for the light, and some semblance of order prevailed. The Marine sergeant, one Timmins, handed me a handful of rags. McCully had a deep wound in the front of his thigh, not bleeding, and several long but shallow cuts on his ribcage. He also had a smashed cheekbone, but it appeared he had not lost too much blood.

Behind me I could hear familiar voices. Sam Dresser was gasping, "He was dripping wet and as white as death, but he told the crew not to kill us-"

An American sailor asked, "Are you saying it was Duco, mate?"

One of the Marines said, "He hit me with his fist-I was kicked by a mule oncet almost as hard-"

Meanwhile it became clear there were other injured men in the dark, men that had been overpowered, and, after being stripped, tossed casually into the hold. There was at least one fracture, several still unconscious, a torn knee, sprains, a broken collarbone.

Yellow Jack was crouched in a corner, a great lump on his forehead, holding his right arm, cursing viciously and steadily. "Jack, what happened?" I asked.

"It was him, and no sperrit, neither.. he twisted me arm almost off and smashed me into the bulkhead, Jim. I'm all right, check the other lads."

A voice came out of the darkness, one of the American Marines. "Men, you know they intend to kill us come morning. Come to peace with your Maker tonight, if you're so inclined."

Another voice, Allan I thought, said quietly, "I'm mortal tired o' bein' locked in the hold."

Schooner

Hispaniola

Chapter 12

The Sorting

All night, the Black Swan sailed steadily, if slowly, on the same course that McCully had set. They roused us late, no water, no food, and lined us up along the midships lee rail, Marines at one end, American sailors in the middle, and Hispaniolas at the other. We blinked in the morning sun; a squalid group in our small-clothes. Lt McCully was unconscious on the deck before us. There were only a few pirates about, none aloft. A small crew was at work forward, rigging the block, tackle and lines to raise and step the foremast, still flat on deck. Lounging against the opposite rail, a half dozen or so men held the Marines' muskets, with fixed bayonets, levelled at us.

Our line began whispering and murmuring. Some of the mates had carried a table and one of de Rijk's outsize chairs onto the deck. A group brought a sailcloth and dumped our clothes and personal items on the table. I worried about the map, in that pile somewhere.

Kapitein Duco de Rijk made his appearance, squinting at the light, bandage around his head, another around his throat, hair and beard wild, and seated himself at the table. I had already seen him and treated him, but he had been lying flat and immobile. Seeing so much meat on the hoof, so to speak, was startling, to say the least. One of the pirate sentries thumped the deck with his musket-stock three times, and all the crew filed silently on deck, including Paulo, limping, and Grimwood the Briton, moving slowly with his thousand stitches. Grimwood took station next to the giant's chair. For some reason the ship's cook and assistant appeared with several buckets of slush and garbage, passed behind us, and began emptying the buckets over the rail.

Duco beckoned Grimwood, who came close, and Duco whispered in his ear. Grimwood began to speak. "Freebooters of the Black Swan-we have lost and regained our vessel-and I have died and become reborn." Another whisper, and Grimwood/Duco continued, "We have before us those that would hang us by the neck until we are dead. We have before us those who killed our shipmates-the sailors and Marines of the rebel American Navy."

One of the mates hurried over to him and spoke in Duco's ear. Duco waved Grimwood away, then began examining each belt, each knife, each pocket in the clothing, methodically tossing items into several separate piles on the deck.

Without looking up, Duco de Rijk spoke aloud for the first time, a deep, urgent, whispered voice with only a trace of Welsh and Dutch: "I am told that some of you were prisoners aboard the American. Step forward." The Hispaniolas looked around at each other nervously, and we each stepped forward hesitantly. Duco continued tossing weapons into one pile, coins into another, ringing on the deck, clothes in another.

He went on, "These Americans have made this crew, honest gentlemen of fortune all, most short-handed. I am not a cruel man. I offer you of the..." The mate whispered in his ear again, "..Hispaniola, the opportunity to join our crew."

Duco paused to bite a gold-piece. He signalled another seaman, who came forward with a pail of seawater, and threw it forcefully on Lt McCully. McCully sputtered and opened his eyes. Several more armed pirates clustered at the far end of the line, next to the Marines.

Duco de Rijk continued, "Do not misunderstand me, Hispaniolas - if you join, you join for life, however long that is. If you do not, you may join the Americans." He motioned, and the pirates seized the Marine at the far end of the line and flung him over the rail backward into the sea. We heard the splash, a silence, and then a long scream. I did not even know this man's name. Duco looked up at this and smiled. I wish he had not. "That is Mynheer Shark and his messmates." Gesturing at the line of men and the various piles of possessions, he went on, "This is our little ceremony. How many times have we done this, my friends?" The pirates smiled and nodded, a few nudging their neighbours.

Still sorting, in a conversational tone, he said, "I am Kapitein Duco de Rijk and this is the Black Swan. You have never heard of us, because that is how we survive and thrive. I do not care about the might of the Royal Navy. I do not care about the infant American Navy. We take what we want from them. We are disguised as a slaver because sailors think they know what a slaver is. That one-" he nodded at McCully, who was trying to sit up, despite his wounds, "-was clever enough to row downwind of us.   Because this ship does not stink, we took broadsides, and it hurt us."

Duco motioned again, and another American Marine was thrown backward over the rail into the sea.   I should have known that man's name as well. This time there was no scream following the splash, but the pirates who had thrown the man were chuckling and pointing, so I assumed the sharks were still on duty.   The heap on the table was dwindling rapidly.   Duco looked at us. "Hispaniolas, I can't say fairer." He resumed sorting. "Join, or die."

I was watching the pile of clothing, small weapons, belts, &c. before Duco, wondering when he would encounter Flint's map; I heard Livesey's last words to me again, praying that may be true.   I was in a most peculiar state-heart slamming my ribs, hearing unnaturally acute, where every slap of wave against the ship was a surfacing shark, wondering whether I would drown before being eaten alive.   At that moment,   one of the American sailors cracked, sobbing and begging for his life, calling out that it was McCully, first and foremost, scrag HIM...   Duco gestured and that nameless sailor went over the side, with a great sobbing scream, cut short in the splash.

Almost in response to the splash, Brighouse was the first to step forward. After a moment of shared looks, Jan and the three remaining Dutch stepped forward.   Then the British stepped forward, all except me.   Allan, Sam, and Yellow Jack all looked back shamefacedly toward me for a moment. Paulo, the little knife-fighter, scurried forward and spoke in Duco de Rijk's ear.   The apostate Hispaniolas walked slowly away from the rest of the prisoners, wanting the geography of the deck to attest to their new allegiance to a life of piracy; not a one of them could look at us.

Duco spoke to me directly. "You. Turn around." I did so, displaying the recently healed stripes on my back, and the pirates laughed and cheered at the sight, doubtless one they knew well. I turned back to Duco, who was grinning, looking down at his sorting. "Paulo says you doctored him and my crew well-and that you are British, not American. I ask only once more, medicoe - join us or die."

I shook my head, wondering why I'd lost my will to live some time in the past week. Duco gestured, and four pirates came to me, seizing my legs and arms, swung me back and forth several times like a sack of meal and flung me over the rail.

Schooner

Hispaniola

Chapter 13.

A Change Of Course

As soon as I surfaced, I struck for the side of the Black Swan, hoping to seize some of the lines and rigging still dangling into the sea. The side of the ship scraped swiftly past me as I sought in vain for some purchase, anything to keep me from the sharks. For a split second I beheld the dark blue eyes and heard the voice of Miss Lilith, Trelawney's daughter. The barnacles on the ship's sides cruelly scraped my hands and forearms.

It was no use - the side of the ship passed me and I was in the open sea behind the Black Swan, looking up despairingly at the great stern window, already moving away. Suddenly I was struck a great blow in the neck and shoulder blades which almost drove me beneath the surface. One hand instinctively reached up and grasped the gunwale of the jolly-boat, being towed behind to grant more space on deck. I fancied I felt the swirl of a shark behind me; this propelled me up and over the side, and I collapsed with a great gasp amidst fishy-smelling tarpaulins and bait buckets.

No sooner did I conceive of burrowing beneath the sailcloth, than I heard a halloa and hubbub from the Black Swan's stern rail; looking up with bleary, salt-stung eyes, I saw the silhouettes of the crew, with the great bulk of Duco the Giant, unmistakable, directly above the rudder-pintles. From their actions it was clear they were going to bring me aboard again - to what end - only to enjoy flinging me to the sharks again?

Once aboard, I could barely stand. Jan and Jack supported me until my legs functioned again. Dripping and shaking, I looked at Duco, trying to ready myself for whatever was to come. Flint's chart of the island was across his little table; Grimwood was pointing excitedly at it, almost dancing, and he with all his wounds.

"Your crewmates -" and he gestured toward the Hispaniolas - "tell me you kept this with you since you all left your ship. Grimwood says it is a treasure map and 'J.F.' is John Flint. Where did you get this map o' John Flint's, Medicoe?"

My mind was racing as it always did in a pinch; best to admit to part of the truth over a complete lie. I took a deep breath. "From Long John Silver himself, your Honour." My voice was shaking. "I was cabin boy on his last voyage, back in sixty-five -- Gave me the map with his own two hands, he did. 'Jim,' says he, 'I never seen a smarter lad. Smart as paint, ye are. Take this here auld map from Long John and keep it for me, matey, and mayhap we'll return to the island for the rest of the blunt.', says he."

"Aye, sounds like Silver," said Grimwood. "Hawkins, you're one of us!"

The Giant's eyes were narrowed. "Just gave it you, eh? Why would he do that?"

"I helped him escape hanging back in England, Captain."

"Where were this 'last voyage'?"

I pointed at the map. "There."

From behind me, I heard Brighouse the Loyal say, hesitantly, "Cap, all us Hispaniolas knew we was on a treasure voyage-just didn't know where to."

"That means, medicoe, that you know the owners or captain of the Hispaniola, am I correct?" Duco was fingering the yellowed map as he spoke.

"No, sir, I do not know them."

Duco was in full barrister mode. "You're lying. You're the friend of that Squire that owes the Dutch. And that Doctor. Hispaniola is on a treasure voyage and you just happen to have a map to treasure. Was Hispaniola headed toward this island?"

"I don't know, Captain. It were a secret."

"You don't know."

I said nothing.

Off to one side, Paleface Ruen the sailing-master had been glaring at me since I was dragged back aboard. In a shockingly loud voice he called, "Roast him, Cap!"

Duco shook his head at that. To me he said, "Ah, you are a hero to die with your American friends, I forgot." He stepped toward me and gently took me by the arm and walked me, still dripping, to the bows, where none could hear. I barely came up to his shoulder. Looking out at sea, he whispered, in his Welsh-Dutch accent, "Hawkins, I see you discovered Duco's secret of continued life - the blessed jolly-boat. However-you could be Silver's long-lost son, I care not. What I want are the bearings to that treasure."

How many men had died, wanting or finding the bearings of that accursed island? Staring at the gently-heaving sea, Duco's huge bulk in the corner of my eye, I said "Captain, I do not know the bearings to the island." My heart sank; it had been said with no conviction whatsoever.

Duco sighed. "Hawkins, many persons have thought that since I am large I must be a stupid. I am not a stupid. I would rather not kill you – again - this ship needs a medicoe. But you will tell me the bearings before we turn around, or at the next anchorage, I will roast McCully alive before you and THERE you will tell me the bearings."

Boldly I said, "Captain, stop throwing the Americans to the sharks and I will tell."

I heard a strange deep snuffling sound and realized Duco was laughing, and he looked down at me. "All right, Medicoe, we can sell them as slaves. Tell me."

I recited the latitude and longitude that Livesey had given me. Duco repeated them, and turned to face the rest of the ship. He called Grimwood closer and said, in his raspy whisper,

"Americans into the hold; get the mast stepped immediately; and set course Northwest by North!"

Turning to me, he said, "And you, Hawkins, are the ship's medicoe, and you will haul on a line when required. Join the crew."

From far below, one of the Americans called, in a plaintive voice, "Hey! What about our clothes?"

*****

Duco de Rijk's crew was undoubtedly a nasty lot of murderers -- but one would never know it from their behaviour with one another and in their ship handling, quite unlike the rebellious, deeply stupid and often drunken pirates who had comprised Silver's crew aboard the Hispaniola. That lot were forever challenging Silver's position and judgement, while this crew seemed thoroughly cowed by Duco. There were no spirits on board, for one thing. Duco would brook no fighting among the men. Indeed, he was so dominant aboard the Black Swan that the crew were quite civil to the newcomers from the Hispaniola, and I prevailed upon Duco to allow me to feed and minister to the American seamen in the hold.

Duco was serious about me continuing as ship's doctor, and as word got around that I was not merely practising upon them, some crewmen with old injuries showed up in sickbay, looking for some relief.

One of them was a villainous looking fellow from the Indian subcontinent, who presented a weeping eye socket. He said his name was Ali, and he insisted on calling me

'Doctor Sahib'. One of his eyes had been badly burned, it appeared, and the wound never quite healed. I asked him how he had got it, and his unhurried, somewhat elliptical discourse was so remarkable that I reproduce it here to the best of my recollection.

"My name is Burraq Ali and my family has lived in Lahore for many generations. My father is a coppersmith and our shop sits near the northern end of Lahore bazaar. I have some schooling, I read and write Urdu and a bit of the Arabic. From very young I worked in my father's shop, tending fires and carrying the pieces to the workers. It is a noisy place, the tapping going on always."

"I remember a disruption in the bazaar. I was very young; because of the stories I thought it was a Hindu mob and feared for my life.   From near the southern gate came a furious shouting, saying sons of whores, sell your mother, why don't you. I crept closer and saw one man only in filthy clothes, pulling down all the stock in Hakim the Rugseller's stall, but where was Hakim?   When the ground was covered with carpets, he stormed right across to my father's shop, shouting abuse and scattering the urns and narghiles and plates all around. My father, normally the aggressive one, had disappeared into the back workroom while this madman, with a long dirty beard, rampaged until every last piece was off the wall. Very noisy indeed. The man stopped suddenly, raised his head as if he heard his name, turned around and left the bazaar at a trot. "

"I ran to my father, who said, help me clean up. When I asked about the man and why, he shook his head and said, watch what happens.   I was quite young, five or six years only, but I still recall the steady stream of customers over the next week. I visited also Hakim's almost empty shop.

No, no dacoits, Hakim laughed, I have not been robbed. I have had the best week in five years, said he, thanks to the Jelali Mahdzub."

"You see, Ali, said my father, every piece the mad one touched is sold. That is why I did not interfere; his visit was a blessing, baraka, from Allah. Father then said, and he is not the only one. I was thinking and thinking, there is more than one of this type of man? This is when I became curious about these fellows. Hakim called them Mahdzubiat, the God-mad ones. Jelali means hot, like fire, or very angry. My father had little more to say, so I went to the Imam of our mosque. He said to me, Ali, these things are outside Shariat, the laws of Islam, and he would say no more."

"On a visit home, my older brother Abdullah, who attended a school down south in Karachi, said he had been told these God-mad ones had gone too far too fast. Too fast for what, I asked, but he just laughed and shook his head. Too far from what, I thought."

"As I grew older, I ventured farther from our shop, and indeed learned the whole of the bazaar. But though I watched and watched for over a year, the God-mad man did not reappear. In this time I had made two best friends, Jamil and Mirzad."

"One day they came to the shop and said Ali, come with us, and we will show you a wonder. We three boys ran to the western outskirts of the town, to the top of a small hill, with a ruined wall. We sat and watched and waited. I grew impatient and called them sons of dogs, but they hushed me and resumed their watch. Here he comes at last, said Jamil. On the road below, along came a small man in grey and brown robes, dirty turban and a staff.

My companions were suppressing laughter and their eyes sparkled with excitement. After the walker passed us, Jamil nodded to Mirzad, who motioned to me to peek over this wall."

"Mirzad whispered, Istafar'Allah, means forgive me God. The man staggered as if he had been struck, and whirled about to see his tormentor, and we hid behind the wall. We peeked again as the man walked on, muttering angrily. Jamil nodded and Mirzad whispered, Allahu Akbar, means God is most great, with the same result. It is like a whip on his flesh, said Mirzad, and for respect he must face the word of God."

"This was indeed a wonder, Doctor Sahib, and only fueled my interest and curiosity about these people. I asked everyone I met, and many people held these God-mad ones in a sort of regard. The Chai stalls were a great place to hear the stories. There was a very poor but famous Murshid whose whole family lived in one room in Karachi for many years. His followers wanted to put him in a palace but he would not let them. Over time people became aware his youngest son was a very special one. When this son was old enough he signed up on an East India merchantman, and would be gone for months at a time. I met a man who had been on Hajj, and who met the Murshid's youngest son there in Mecca, and visited with him; but telling this upon his return he was mocked by persons who knew for a fact that this son's ship was in the middle of the Pacific Ocean at that very same time. So here is a high one that can be in two places at once."

"I could not get enough of these miracle stories. My friends mocked me, calling me O Seeker of Saints, but I did not care."

"Several years passed by, and one Friday I was in mosque with my father and brothers for Al-Asr prayers; we were saying Rakats. I became aware of a feeling on my cheek, one side of my face. I looked around, but just saw the line of men performing Du'a while reciting. Several weeks later, at mosque again, I had this same feeling on the right side of my face. It was stronger this time, like finding a warm stove in a cold room with your eyes closed. I was almost at the end of the row; there was one man only to my right. I peeked at him, a slender fellow with a red beard, my father's age or perhaps younger, dark robe, clean turban, quite respectable."

"The heat on my face remained until we finished our prayers. All the men were in a queue to file out when I saw my friend Jamil was next to me. For such a mocker, Jamil was very well-informed about these saintly fellows. Indicating the dark robed man, I asked Jamil if he knew him. He grinned and said, O Seeker of Saints, this one is known as Qizil Baba, and is a reputed Sufi, a one-hundred percent high one, a perfect target for your persecutions. He lives somewhere in Seramwalla district, said Jamil."

"Qizil Baba, I thought, red bearded father; red is the colour of the Prophet's hair, peace be upon him. I had chores to do at home so I could not slip away, but another time, Friday month of Rajab, I followed the Baba after mosque. This Qizil Baba was no Mahdzub, very quiet and polite. I had been told this man was a Ghaus; now Ghaus means helper or helper of the God, but it had another meaning, but no one would tell. I remembered always this heat on my face, so I followed him from mosque, a very curious young fellow indeed."

"It was a long walk. Qizil Baba stopped at a food stall. I followed as close as I dared. He walked right through the

Seramwalla district, past the edge of town. All the time he was chanting Zikr. Allah, Allah, Allahu Akbar, tapping his stick in time. The farther he got from the town, the louder was this Zikr. I was far behind him and still could hear."

"Qizil Baba turned off the main path and up a hillside, where I saw a rough hut. He walked to the door of this hut and went inside. I crept up to the window. As I got closer I heard more voices inside, like he joined a prayer group or something similar. I peeked in the corner of the window and I saw the hut was bare, no furniture, nothing, no people even. All the time the voices in Zikr. It took a moment for my eye to adjust, and I didn't see anyone standing in the room. I looked down at the floor and there it was."

"Now I tell you, Doctor Sahib, I swear upon the Prophet that this is true. First I saw his face, eyes open, looking right at me, saying Allah, Allah. But then I saw, and this is when I wet my pants, his body was lying several feet away from the head. And the hands had fallen off the arms, the feet from the legs, and every part of the body was saying loud, Allah, Allah. First I thought someone has murdered him. But I could still hear the murmur of Zikr voices, so how can he be dead, saying Allah?"

"But as I looked at this person in pieces on the floor, a light grew like staring in the sun, and it did not stop, and was like a stab in my eye. I fell down and crawled away from the hut into some bushes, to shake and vomit, and I became dead to the world for some time."

"I was in much pain when I woke up. It was dark, and I could not see out of this eye. I stumbled to the hut and opened the door but Qizil Baba al-Ghaus was gone. This is how I learned that Ghaus means a saint whose body falls apart in ecstasy of God.   And what no one told me is that anyone seeing a Ghaus doing this will go blind."

He concluded, "That is how it happened."

I was silent for some time, thinking about miracles in this modern age of science.   Finally I said, "Ali, as a young man you were devout and vitally interested in the miracles of saints and men of God."

He rocked his head in what I took for assent.

"It is difficult for me to reconcile that with your presence on this ship, murdering seamen for money."

He looked away for a moment.   "I am a very bad man.   I have murdered.   I was with a pirate Lascar fleet in the East Indies when taken by the Portuguese; since I am a good gunner and swordsman, they let me live.   They came to this ocean, and now I am with Captain Duco.   I do not know if ever I will see India again."   In a strong, angry voice, he went on,   "Doctor Sahib, in the religion of my fathers, Allah is described as 'Al-Rahman, Ar-Rahim', means the Compassionate, the Merciful.   When I ran weeping to the house of my father, and then to a local Hakim, or doctor, they found my eye was gone as if by a red-hot poker.   Tell me what mercy or compassion was shown to a boy only curious about lovers of God?"

He paused.   "That day I became an enemy of God."

At that moment Paulo, who was becoming more and more mobile, scuttled crabwise into sickbay.   "Doctor!   The sailing-master done for the first mate!"

I ran on deck, pushing through the crowd to Paleface Ruen, sitting on the deck, leaning against the rail. He was bloody to the elbows, holding his right forearm. There was a huge splash of blood on the deck. It was not his. Ruen's wound proved to be a fleabite scratch.

"Who were you fighting with?" I asked.

"First mate Couevel," he said, looking not at me, but at Duco, striding along the maindeck.

With one huge hand, Duco dragged him to his feet.

"Where is Couevel?"

Ruen jerked his thumb at the sea behind him. Duco growled, "I should cripple you for this. There's no fighting on my ship. So now you think you're going to be sailing master AND first mate." He looked around at the crew, all carefully expressionless. "Come to my cabin, dog." And Duco dragged Ruen aft.

Schooner

Hispaniola

Chapter 14

Ashore on Treasure Island

It was late afternoon and the sun was low in the sky when the island was sighted, just a dim irregular outline on the horizon. Our goal was the North Inlet, being closest to the theoretical silver cache. This required we circle the island clockwise. Above me the sails snapped and crackled in the trade-wind. We were coming from east-southeast, and Sailing-master Ruen took us toward the west shore. The low cliffs of Haulbowline Head drifted past on our starboard side, about a half-mile away. The hands not aloft were lining the starboard railing, hungrily watching the land go past.

The Black Swan was just abreast of Mizzenmast Hill when the wreck was sighted. it was quite dim at first, but you could see the outline of the stern against the light hill-side. When we got closer we could see it was a small ship, stern in the air, nose down among the rocks, masts down. Sam Dresser was the first to recognise her - it was the old Hispaniola, dead like so many others in this place. I stood at the railing, with anguish in my heart, and watched the wreck go by. The schooner's foremast had gone, her sails were rags, and her bowsprit and stem were buried in the surf. Perhaps a dockyard could have brought her up, but of dockyards we had none.

Above all, I wondered if Livesey and Trelawney lived. About a quarter mile past the wreck was a small beach area - if they swam with the current, it was possible they emerged from the sea just there. There were no signs of life but I knew a short uphill tramp to the northeast would lead to Ben's cave. Duco knew naught of Ben's cave; it was not on Flint's map, of course, and I had not volunteered its existence.

The tumble and heave of the sea calmed as soon as the Black Swan passed into the mouth of the island's North Inlet, between the green hills into the shadows of dusk. The leadsman was chanting in the bows, but I knew in my every dream that the sea-floor shoaled about a mile inland, with about another mile of shallow water to the beach and then the path up to Ben Gunn's cave. If the Squire and Doctor were still alive, they would take shelter there.

It turned full dark, with a little way still on the ship, and Paleface Ruen had lanthorns hung fore and aft. Loosing a line down the larboard side of the ship, I slipped over the side during the stamp-and-heave and splashing of the anchor, and struck for the southeastern shore of the inlet. It was midsummer in the West Indies, and the salt water was warm as blood. The waves crept ashore like pirates with knives in their teeth.

I reckoned I had until morning before Duco sent an expedition to the island to find me, assuming he cared. My life was forfeit only if the silver was not there, or if it was; the Doctor and the Squire were my immediate concern. The sea-breeze coming up the channel kept my wet clothes cool; I was happy to keep moving up the hillside, moving around the shoulder of the hill toward Ben's cave.

I reached a flat grassy spot and was walking briskly when I heard a loud, breathy, sobbing snort from the woods to my right. It was so unexpected that I froze. There had been no large animals save goats on the island when I was there previously, and that was no goat. I stared at the dark until there were dots before my eyes. I could see nothing, but could hear the rustling and footfalls of a very large creature moving toward me. When the long face and huge dark eyes coming at me became visible, I almost screamed before I realized it was a horse! A light-coloured horse, which ambled up to me, and stood next to me, as if inviting a caress. I bent over and plucked some grass and the horse took it from my hand, its lips tickling my palm, and then it bent its head to graze. I spent a couple of minutes with this warm, friendly creature, wondering how it got there - of course, shipwrecked, not so long ago as to become wild, and I wondered if there were more on the island. But patting of horses was not my purpose that night. So I took my leave.

When I got there, the cave mouth was dark and uninviting. No one responded to my calls. There was no flint or steel, so I spent the night dozing sitting and shivering in my sea-damp clothes, just inside the cave mouth, next to the small trickling spring-fed creek. At first light I creaked upright and moved into the recesses of Ben's cave, and took a drink from the spring. I found day-old breadfruit, remnants of a fire, a huge old stew-kettle, a shovel, and firewood - it was clear that someone, I prayed it was Livesey and Trelawney, had been there as recent as the day before.

The only other shelter on the island was the blockhouse up the hill from the southern anchorage. I set off down the valley, about a five or six mile walk in the cool early morning. There were traces of horses about - more than just my friendly ghost of the previous night.

Down in the valley, headed south, I rounded the shoulder of Spyglass hill on my left, the early morning sunlight on the hillside above me. Birds were twittering and the distant boom of surf on the east shore were the only sounds. It occurred for the very first time that this island was actually quite beautiful; if I were a reclusive sort, one could do worse than live here, like Mr Defoe's Crusoe, only with money. And a small and stout ship. And plenty of pigs and goats. And instead of a man Friday, a brown-limbed, beautiful girl with bright eyes... enough of that. I was walking along a natural path or corridor, and as the light got better I could see hoof-prints, but, oddly, they were all headed my way, south toward the stream mouth and Capt. Kidd's Anchorage. I wished I had the reputed tracking skills of an Indian from the Colonies; the wily Rapahannock, the Iroquois. I should have asked the Americans if any of them had met a red Indian. All I was doing was ignoring my hunger. Ahead was the hillside leading up to Flint's block-house.

I climbed quietly and came up on the back corner of the log compound. A gentle breeze rustled the trees, and clouds scudded overhead. Some of the logs in the wall had fallen over, and I climbed through a gap into the clearing. I circled the building, listening and watching. The iron kettle which encircled the bubbling spring had completely rusted through. I took several long drinks of sandy water before coming up for air.   Coming around to the front porch I could see that the roof of the block-house had fallen in: understandable, in that this structure was made by Flint's men probably thirty years before.   But it was not deserted - for, leaning against one of the porch posts, was a leather bag.   I picked it up and examined it - well-cured and finished, I had never seen it before.   There was stale bread inside, which I immediately started eating, looking around wildly for the owner.   Exercising some of those American Indian powers of observation, I noted that the someone had opened a gate in the palisade's south wall, and that there were footprints in the sand, leading in and out of the compound.

Still chewing, I darted for the gate and headed down toward the Anchorage.   Before I reached the crest of the last rise, I heard the whinny of horses.   I moved off the path about 30 yards and, on my belly, crawled to the edge and looked out toward the Anchorage.   I saw a three-masted, squat ship, rigging somewhat ahoo, moored fore and aft about fifty yards off shore.   There were men aboard and men aloft, and, looking down on the beach, I could see part of an enclosure for horses.   They were here capturing horses, and doing some rigging.   I could see several tents at the edge of the treeline, and to my right there were several ship's boats with casks beached next to the mouth of the fresh water stream, so they were watering as well.

Were they pirates?   Spaniards?   A better sailor than myself would have immediately recognised the ship; I did not know until a breeze lifted the flag, red quarters with castles and white quarters with lions.   Or perhaps it was horses.   Definitely Spanish Royal Navy.   Fed and no longer thirsty, I decided to stay where I was and watch.   I could smell smoke from a cook's fire, and a bit of chatter coming from beyond the horse compound. Two men trudged past me on the way to the boats. They pushed one into the water and shipped oars, waiting. From my left came a file of men, Kapitein von Loendersloot in his black coat, First Mate Laemmers, and the Doctor and Squire, followed by two sailors with pistols. My heart was pounding and I wanted to shout, "You're alive!" Livesey and Trelawney looked a bit drawn, but healthy. Their hands were not bound, but it was clear they were prisoners. They all got into the boat, which pulled for the ship.

I waited until they were aboard and taken below before I stole away back toward the cave. Greedily gobbling the breadfruit, I collapsed on a bed of moss and fell deeply asleep.

"Mynheer Medicoe - wakker maken - " I sat up with a start. Duco the Giant was crouched before me. He motioned, and turned to the mouth of the cave. I shaded my eyes. It was mid-morning, and members of the pirate crew were ambling about the clearing in front of the cave, including Sam Dresser and Allan, who gave me a shy nod.

Duco looked down and wagged the packet containing Flint's map at me. "This is that island, and you will take me to the silver now."

All those years ago, after the mutineers were put down, I spent most of my time in the cave, counting and sorting. I had been to the silver burial site only once with Livesey, before he dug it back up with Abe Gray's help. I recalled it was on the far side of Foremast Hill. Paleface Ruen walked up to Duco and myself, fingering the foot-long dirk on his belt. Duco looked at him and said, "He will take us."

I nodded and said, "Captain, there is something you should know. There is a Spanish ship in the south anchorage, here watering and capturing horses. And my friends are with them."

Duco said, "Prisoners?" I nodded. "How many? And which are your friends?"

I said, "Only four survived the wreck - Kapitein Jos von Loendersloot, first mate Jan Laemmers, and my friends, Doctor Livesey and Squire Trelawney, owners of the Hispaniola."

"More Dutch, eh? I will think about this as we find this silver. How many Spanish?"

"About fifty, I think, most on the ship, re-rigging, the rest on the shore. They have some horses, but they haven't caught them all. There might be more hunting-parties."

Duco said, "Not many for a warship. Perhaps these are special horses they hunt."

The three of us circled Ben's hill and headed northeast along the side. It was rough going. For some reason, I kept remembering that day long ago, tugged along like a dog on a leash, with pirates who longed to cut my throat, on the way to an empty hole in the ground.

Around the shoulder of Foremast Hill, to the north shore of the island, on a slope with a stunning view of the Caribbean, we found our own empty hole in the ground. There were two long narrow cases, recently excavated, fresh dirt spilled all around. Paleface Ruen leaped in the hole and tore back the lid of one, showing cut layers of oiled canvas, with something shining inside. Ruen tugged, and came up with a forty-year-old flintlock musket with a short barrel - a boarding weapon. He cocked the empty old gun, pointed it at me and pulled the trigger. He turned his head to Duco and said, "He's lying. Look at this - he got here last night and moved it all. Roast him."

I said to Duco, "It was here thirteen years ago. Look again - that's several days old."

Duco was in a study, looking out at the ocean. He looked like a Viking considering which town to sack next. After a long two minutes, he said, "We will take the Spaniard by sea tonight and on land at first light. Perhaps we can save your Squire and Doctor. Perhaps they know where this silver is." He paused. "Perhaps they took it."

Not a word was spoken during the return to the cave.

When we arrived at the cave mouth, Duco said to Paleface Ruen, "Sailing-master, take the ship out of sight over the horizon and return here just at dusk. We will take the boats around to this bay and take the Spaniard quietly in the dark. We will give the shore party grapeshot at first light. Go now."

With only a few barked orders, it was so - Duco gave the four sailors directions to the cache of muskets, and Ruen and the rest headed for the boats and the Black Swan.

I was dozing in the sun at the cave entrance. Walking up, Duco said, "We will go see this ship of yours."

After a mouthful of water and taking more breadfruit from the cave, Duco and I set off for the Spanish ship and encampment. As we walked beneath the trees, I ventured a question.

"Captain, what stops Master Ruen from simply marooning you and taking the Black Swan himself? He doesn't strike me as quite trustworthy."

The Giant snuffled in what I now knew to be his laughter. "Yes, he's a knife man. The crew doesn't trust him, either. He cut up a few before I put a stop to that. But he's a good sailor and he knows navigation. Loyalty - these rats never saw as much money as on my ship. No women, no fighting, and no spirits.... but you should see them when we moor in a friendly port - they slide down the cables to get ashore - and most of them can't even swim!"

"I've never heard of any ship, merchantman, Royal Navy, or pirate, that didn't have its grog ration and a spirit-room," I said.

He looked sideways down at me and said simply, "The Black Swan is my ship."

I subsided for a while.

We made our way to the blockhouse and thus to my lookout-point. Duco and I squirmed like savages through the brush to the edge of the hill. Duco watched the encampment and the ship with avid interest. He said quietly to me, "Your friends are locked below. Spaniards will ransom anyone anytime; if that does not work, your friends will be sold into New Spain as plantation slaves. I'll get them out alive -- they may know where the silver is."

With that, in the company of the most dangerous man I'd ever seen, I fell asleep in the shade.

Schooner

Hispaniola

Chapter 15

The Night Expedition

Ten miles doesn't sound so far. One could walk it, on level ground, in three hours. Less than one hour on a fast horse. Ten miles rowing a boat in the open ocean, against the tradewinds, is another matter.

Paleface Ruen turned from his station in the bow of the longboat. He hissed, "Pull, you dogs - put your backs into it!"

We did. We were pulling straight south, along the eastern shore of the island. It was a moonless and cloudless warm summer night; I could see the dark profile of the island on our right, bobbing up and down with the waves. There were four boats all told, each laden with edged weapons. Duco's hand-picked crew were far in the lead, all of us headed for the Spaniard moored in Capt. Kidd's Anchorage on the south side of the island. Every minute or so a spiff of broached wave splattered all hands, so we were soon drenched and chilly. Near my feet were a small sword, as close as I could find to a fencing sword, and a heavy bent iron pry-bar. For I intended to find the Squire and the Doctor, doubtless locked belowdecks on the Spanish ship.

"How many do you think'll be aboard?" said Brighouse.

"Save your breath, mate," said Sam Dresser. "It's still a long pull."

"Not many," said one of Duco's crew. "Any seaman'd sleep ashore if he could."

Sam said, "That's why we're carrying that heavy little b_____d." For each of the ship's boats carried a squat little keg of grapeshot.

Eventually, on our right, we saw the Skeleton Island rock, which guarded the Anchorage, and we began to circle it. The sea calmed and the wind abated. Ruen ordered oars shipped and the oarlocks padded. We dipped oars again and continued. The other boats were invisible, as they should be. My back ached, my palms burned, and there were splinters in my backside.

We soon rounded the rock, well into the Anchorage, and there was the Spanish three master, dim lanthorns hanging over the bows and quarterdeck, and one over the stern rail. She was moored side on to the shore. We were well within earshot. Craning my neck I could now see Duco's other three boats, the one carrying Duco in the lead. Ruen raised his hand, and we all stopped rowing, dead in the water. I twisted around to see better. No one was visible on the ship's deck, which made sense - it was well after midnight, more likely around 2 AM. Duco's lone boat rowed silently up to her port side near the stern, and it disappeared in the shadow cast by the ship's side.

My eyes adjusted, and I could see one slender figure climb the ship's side and stop just below the rail. He had a line around his waist, and slowly raised a boarding-net with hooks, which he affixed to the top of the rail. The boat's crew, led by Duco, silently swarmed up the ship's side on the net, and I could see them slip over the rail one by one. To my amazement, Paulo, the cut-up little knife-fighter, was one of the first over the rail.

The second boat's crew headed for the bow, and performed the same silent operation with their own boarding net. There were sixteen or more heavily-armed pirates aboard her now, and not a sound was to be heard.

Paleface Ruen the sailing-master raised his right hand, and we rowed to our place, nudging Duco's boat forward, and began retrieving our weapons. I had the line already wrapped around my neck, and I hastily tied a slip-knot over my sword pommel and my pry-bar, and slung them over my back as I stood.

Ruen, halfway up the net, whispered to the boat crew, "You make a sound and I'll skin ye."

I was so stiff from sitting and rowing that clambering up that spongy, springy net was quite a feat. As I came over the rail, my pry-bar came loose, and I caught it just before it clanged on the deck. Ruen was there next to the rail, crouched down so none ashore could see. He motioned each of us down. Of course I wished to shed no blood; my sole idea was to free my friends, whom I suspected would be imprisoned in a cabin area on one of the lower decks. I scanned the upper deck in the dim light and saw there were fore and aft companionways, leading to the deck below us.

Ruen gave the signal to move aft, so I let the boat crew pass me, and then I scuttled over to the fore companionway and, laying flat, hung my head below. There was only one lanthorn lit for the entire foredeck; more shadow than light. However, it was silent, so I crept down the stairs and commandeered the lanthorn. There were cabins and galley; I knew I had to go deeper. A noise made me whirl. At the far end of the deck I could see some of Duco's men milling about with their own lanthorn; one saw me and waved.

Another stairwell beckoned, this to the gundeck no doubt. I gathered that Duco and his men were hunting Spaniards in the aft cabins, which suited me fine. There was one more fore companionway on the deserted gundeck. I wrinkled my nose; the Spanish were none too clean in their sanitation and washing, apparently. Or perhaps that was just the smell from the bilges drifting up. I descended this last stairwell, and found myself on a sort of orlop deck. I was in among cable-tiers and store-rooms, carrying my sword and pry-bar in one hand, the lanthorn on the other. I entered a passageway, set the light down, and tapped on each locked door in succession. Silence.

Gathering my light, I hurried toward the stern, passing sailrooms and the pump room. There was an open space, bounded by a series of closed cabin doors. Bread room. Steward's room. Purser's cabin, slop room, marine clothing, block room, another sail room. One was locked. Muffled voices from behind. "Livesey, is that you?" I called.

"It's us," came from behind the door. I smashed the lock and doorjamb and Livesey and Trelawney were there. "Jim, lad! How fine to see you!" cried Livesey. Trelawney grasped me by the shoulders and said nothing. They were both fairly dressed, but worn-looking.

"We're rescued!" said Trelawney, at last.

"Not exactly," I replied. "This ship has been taken by one Duco de Rijk, a pirate. The Hispaniolas joined his crew - it was that or the sharks."

"Pirates, eh?" Livesey eyed my sword and pry-bar. He extended his hand for the pry-bar. He looked aft. "I don't need the lanthorn. There's something I must do with no delay. Will you two be alright?" And with that he was gone, running toward the stern. I hadn't seen him run in many years.

"Water, Jim," said the Squire. "We thought you were dead."

"Me, too, more than once. Let's find you some."

Back up two decks to the galley, and fresh water for the both of us. There was nothing to do but go back down to the gundeck, where Duco's crew were milling about the cannon. All gunports were closed tightly, cannons reeved into place. Still carrying my lanthorn, we walked up to the crew. Little Paulo's knife hand automatically came up at the sight of the Squire, like a dog on point. I said, "This is my friend Squire Trelawney. Duco wants him kept safe, you understand?" The knife disappeared.

Paleface Ruen made his way to my side. "Only three Spaniards aboard, more's the luck. Found your Dutch captain and his mate, should be along." He looked at the Squire. "Thought there were two on 'em, not one."

I said, "There is another, I think he had the flux, he can't go anywhere." Ruen nodded. At that moment Livesey casually walked out of the darkness. He had lost my pry-bar somewhere. I said, "This is the other of my friends."

Duco's men sorted themselves into guncrews. Livesey and Trelawney sat down out of the way, and I was pressed to be one of the powder-boys. I said to Ruen, "I think I know where the powder-room is, down one deck in the stern."

"Go ahead." To the others he said, "We need two loads for eight guns. Quiet, now."

Me and my light in the lead, I retraced my steps to the orlop deck and passed the open cabin door where my friends had been kept. We opened every other door until we found ourselves at a larger door at the stern. "This has to be it," I said to the others. But the door was locked from the inside. Some strong boots finally broke the lock.

There was a light inside - unexpected. We crowded in the door to see a sweating, panicked Spanish sailor standing on a tier of powderkegs, holding a naked torch. He had spilled black powder all over the kegs and deck. He croaked, in Castellano, "Detenganse! Oh nos vuelo al diablo!" It took no translator for us. We all froze, holding out placating hands, and started to back out of the room.

Ruen pushed through the little knot of hands, and faced the Spaniard, who was shaking the torch alarmingly. Ruen half-turned as if to speak to us, and his right hand whipped at blinding speed -- the Spaniard had a knife in his throat, gurgling his life away. He began to topple, and I launched myself toward the torch, landing flat on the deck as it dropped into my left hand. Ruen came forward and took the torch out of my hand, and handed it to one of the crew at the door. "Well caught," he said.

Back to the gunroom with the powder, I saw that the guncrews were ready with the kegs of grapeshot. They eased each of the cannon back in their trucks, and loaded. Laemmers and von Loendersloot were there, observing. The night was not over, so we each took our ease as best we could, once again between cannon.

A 'hist' woke me, and the guncrews were silently opening the gunports on the starboard, or shore, side.   All lanthorns were out. It was only slightly lighter out than in, but I could see the crews straining to shift the mighty beasts silently, each aimed for a light-coloured tent pitched under the treeline. Duco was among them, barely able to stand upright, even between the crosstimbers, quietly supervising and helping shift the cannon. At this range, less than one hundred yards, they could not possibly miss, especially with grapeshot.

One of the crew came from the bows with a slow-match. Each of the gun-captains came forward with his own, and got a light. The ship rocked slightly on the morning tide.

The roar of eight cannon shattered the dawn silence.   A great hubbub arose from the swamp to our left, and I imagined thousands of sea-birds taking to the air.

One more ragged broadside and it was over. The neat tents in a neat row along the trees were now shredded piles of cloth. The horses had broken loose from their pen at the first broadside and were long gone.   Two Spanish ran down the beach, cut down immediately by Duco's men in the trees.

I was still peering out a gunport when Paleface Ruen came over to me. "Duco says to wait for him on deck."

Livesey, Trelawney and I emerged on deck in the early dawn. Duco joined us a moment later. Duco said to Livesey, "Doctor, I believe you know Hawkins, our medicoe?"

"Medicoe, eh? Yes, I do."

"Then perhaps you know where the silver is, " said Duco.

"Captain, I know the silver is missing. However, I believe that we might find it. Would you grant Hawkins here, the Squire and myself two days to find it?" said the Doctor.

Duco considered for a moment, looking around at the sky and at the Spaniards' shredded tents. "No. You have until sundown. Find it and live. Go now."

Schooner

Hispaniola

Chapter 16

Discovery Of The Treasure

It was late morning before we made it to the beach. Having dumped the dead Spanish from the ship into the sea off Skeleton Island, Duco's men had collected all the boats at the shoreline. With a clumsy, ghastly gaiety which made me suspect some of them had got at the Spaniard's spirits, the pirate crew were busily stripping the bodies of the Spaniards killed ashore of all weapons, clothes and jewellery, after which the bodies were flung into the boats, to soon join their shipmates offshore.

Livesey, Trelawney and I tramped inland, into the blessed shade and coolness of the forest. Livesey led us to a stand of breadfruit trees. While picking and stuffing our pockets, he ventured mildly, "That Captain Duco certainly is... large."

Trelawney said, "How extraordinary. I didn't notice any horses. Livesey, earlier, did you see horses?"

I was too sickened and numb from the night's slaughter for their jokes. We continued toward Ben's cave. After a few minutes Livesey stopped, removed his coat, pulled up his shirtwaist in back and extracted a bulky leather brief of some sort.

He turned off the path and gestured for us to follow, and he found a little grassy clearing, well sheltered. He sat crosslegged and started pulling packets out of the brief. He opened one, a heavy paper map, and flattened it on the ground.

"These were rolled up," said Livesey, "and I hope I haven't damaged them too badly. Look, here's all the West Indies, and the top of Spanish America. Let's see.. Porto Rico - Antigua, I think that's Dutch - Bassetere.."

The Squire, looking exhausted, seemed to lack the energy to even sit down; still, there was enough of the man left to be irritated. "What do we care about maps, Livesey? That giant devil still wants our silver, and unless we produce same we are dead men!" He scratched here and there and grumbled, "Bedbugs and fleas; that's what a stay with a Spaniard is good for."

I had collapsed to Livesey's left, leaned over and squinted at the map to see the lines of latitude and longitude. Anticipating me, Livesey leaned forward and put his forefinger on a spot in the ocean just south of Tortola Isle.

"We are here, approximately," he said. "Look - the Spaniards, at least, know about this island; they wrote 'Isla de los Caballos' - I gather that would be Island of the Horses." Looking up at the Squire, he said, "I have two things in mind right now, Trelawney, and we need to gather every wit we possess. First, these are maps from the

Spanish Navy. The Spanish have been using this area as their private ocean for two and a half centuries. Their knowledge of the geography of this area is unsurpassed."

Trelawney seated himself with a grunt and said, "Livesey, our lives are forfeit and you are pottering with maps. I wonder at you."

Smiling, Livesey said, "You have no idea how much these maps would be worth to the Admiralty. If we had the time I would recount the stories of stolen and copied early maps which led the Italian Columbus to attempt his voyages to the East Indies.. he encountered some obstacles, as you know."

"If we live and if we escape to England, Livesey; that money is theoretical, compared to our lives."

Folding the map and gathering his things, the Doctor said "You are in the right of it. First things first, eh? Gentlemen, let's go find some silver. Oh, look! More amanita muscaria." He crouched, looking at a large colony of white mushrooms growing under a log. "I heard of these fungi from a colleague who has studied the various native tribes in Spanish America. They are called 'Flesh Of The Gods'. Amazing tales of ritual use. There's quite a bit growing here."

Trelawney said, "Fascinating. May we go?"

We resumed our leisurely walk back to the cave. I kept an eye behind us, in case von Loendersloot or any of Duco's men should have followed us. As we walked, I talked to the Squire and Doctor. I'd been thinking hard during that long night.

I said, "We left here thirteen years ago and abandoned three of the mutineers, I can't recall their names to mind... you two have been here some days. Is there any sign of them?"

Livesey said, "The mutineers are long gone - no traces, no bones. I conclude they escaped."

The Squire asked, "In what? They must have made a vessel with --- what tools were left here?"

Livesey said, "There were some rusty tools - adze, axe, shovel -"

"Enough to excavate our silver and to make a raft, at least. Now, there are only two places on the island to build and launch a raft," I said, "- Capt. Kidd's Anchorage, which we just left, and the headwaters of the North Inlet. Both have nearby forest."

Livesey broke in, "The silver was buried on the north end near Foremast Hill.. so the raft must have been built near the North Inlet and launched from its beach."

We had just entered the valley of shade next to the Spyglass hill. It was a beautiful, warm day. The trees were thick around us as we followed a natural path along the base of the hill. I heard a nicker from behind us and whirled. There, trotting up to us, tail held high, was my friend of the night. She came up and nosed my shoulder.

The Squire burst out laughing, and said, "What do we have here? Upon my word, James, you have an admirer! What is her name?"

I grinned, stroking her coarse mane and nose. "I wonder if she could be ridden. If we get out of here, I'm taking her with us."

Livesey said, "Well, she's free of the Spaniard, that's certain. There must be thirty horses free again on the island -- she won't lack for company."

Gulping, I smacked her rump, hard, and she trotted off with a reproachful snort. Looking after her, I said, "So our hypothesis is that the three mutineers excavated the silver, built a raft, and launched from the headwaters of the North Inlet. Doctor, what would you estimate the bar silver weighed?"

"The bar silver, all together, was several hundredweight. The bars were merely piled in the hole," he replied.

"That raft would have to be quite large and stable.. and if they were impatient and launched across the incoming tide, they may well have spilled," I said.

We passed the steep rise to the top of Spyglass Hill, on our left.

Livesey said, "That's settled, then. We know where to look. Let us apply ourselves to the larger question - how does a small unarmed group prevail over a much larger armed one?"

"With our minds, of course," I offered.

"I was thinking of a nice stew," said Livesey.

"Upon my word," said the Squire, "for such a slender fellow, you are ruled by your stomach."

As we walked among the trees toward the beach at the head of the North Inlet, we discussed other aspects of our situation, with Duco firmly in control of the island and both ships.; I apprised the Doctor and Squire of the imprisonment of the Americans, and my opinions of the attitudes of the various Hispaniolas who had joined Duco. The Doctor related some of his reflections regarding the island and some well-considered thoughts regarding our prospects. In short, we concocted a plan which might conceivably secure our freedom.

At the edge of the treeline, we split up, one at the head and one on each side of the inlet. We could just see the stern of the Black Swan, moored fore and aft almost a mile down the North Inlet, which was far too shallow for much of its length for a three-master's draft. I clambered on the hillside, swatting at mosquitos and flies, feeling the pangs of hunger. I'd eaten nothing since the previous day's breadfruit and stale bread. I looked up; the day had begun clouding over; we were in for some rain.

Across the water, I heard Trelawney's shout - "I say, Livesey, look here!" When I arrived, ten minutes later, we were among the trees on the north-west shore of the inlet, Trelawney was taking his ease in the shade near a number of tree-stumps, and Livesey was stalking around this little clearing, counting stumps and looking around.

Pointing toward the water, Livesey told Trelawney, "... and it's clear they dragged the logs out through that opening, and built the raft there, above the high-tide mark." He looked back at the clearing, and said, "But I swear they didn't cut enough to-" Suddenly he bolted for the water, and I followed, and could hear Trelawney huffing to his feet behind me. When I reached him,

Livesey was well down toward the low tide line, peering closely at the water. He said to me, "We could use one of Duco's boats, but they are all at the Anchorage, and that would take hours, and the tide would be in by then."

Standing up to his ankles in sandy muck, he looked at me and back at the water. "James, how good a swimmer are you?"

I could see what he was about. I headed back to the high-tide mark and stripped to my smalls, and trudged back through the sand and into the water, which was warm and quite calm. Possibly because of the strong tide, or because of the fresh water flowing into it, this end of the inlet was remarkably clear and free of sargasso. Now over my head, I paddled along, watching the floor of the lagoon as well as I could, staying to the middle of the channel, reasoning the mutineers would want to stay clear of the shallow sides. The water was clear and the bottom was sand; my mind's eye could still see Israel Hands lying against his victim O'Brien's body, in twenty feet of water, all those years before.

When I tired, I rested, floating on my back. Livesey and Trelawney had retired to the shade at the edge of the tree-line, and were watching me intently. Rain began to fall lightly.

Back and forth I swam, trying to be systematic in my coverage of this end of the inlet. Salt water was stinging my eyes, and I decided to take a break, and headed for the northwest shore. I was splashing along, and saw a glimpse of green beneath me. It was strange to swim in the rain - a world of water. The tide was turning, and the surface was a bit ruffled from light wind and rain, so I took a deep breath and dived, eyes open. There was a mound of green moss swaying gently, in about fifteen feet of water. I reached the top of the mound and scraped away the moss, expecting only rock or coral. My fingers wiped across something smooth. Excitedly, I grasped and tugged with both hands, and came away with an oblong, heavy, squarish piece of something; almost out of air, I frantically kicked for the surface and for the shore. When my feet touched, I threw the block toward the shore.

Livesey and Trelawney came running through the rain. Knee-deep in the water, Livesey fished my prize out and wiped off the moss. It was a dull-grey, graphite colour, but definitely metal, not stone. Holding the block in one hand, Livesey drew a long scratch on its surface using one of his brass coat buttons.

We looked at one another, and in one voice, shouted, "Silver!"

We took shelter under the trees while I dressed. Livesey said, "Of course, their raft dumped in the surf; most sailors not being swimmers, they probably righted it and continued their voyage. We have a choice right now. If we hide this ingot in the trees or back in the water, it sounds as if this Duco might spare our lives and ransom us in Spanish America. Possibly. Or, we can announce our find to Duco and proceed as we discussed."

Trelawney and I looked at each other. I shook my head, thinking of all Duco's victims 'lost' at sea. Livesey said, "And I estimate we have seven minutes to decide - look." He pointed to the lagoon, and through the light rain, we could just see one of the Black Swan's longboats heading our way.

"Coming for us or Ben's cave, no matter, my life isn't worth much without that treasure," said the Squire, looking at the both of us, "but yours are. I think our plan is our best chance. Jim, how do you feel about it?"

"I agree." And with that I danced out onto the beach, the very picture of exuberance, waving my arms and shouting to the rowers in the longboat, "Over here!"

Duco was indeed aboard the ship's boat, as were Sam Dresser and Allan. Apparently having completed some phase of plundering the dead and the captured Spanish ship, Duco had returned to the Black Swan via the sea. As he splashed toward the shore, I ran toward him with the ingot, saying, "Captain! We found it!"

Duco, hair plastered down, dripping wet in the warm rain, hefted the silver bar in one huge paw. "Where is the rest?"

I pointed. "Right out there, in fifteen feet of water, but the tide's coming in. I need some help to get it, right away."

Duco turned to the sailors, who had grounded the longboat, saying, "Who can swim?" Several sailors indicated they could. We walked to the shore closest to the cache.

I said to the group, "It's about fifty yards out, a big green mound about fifteen feet down." The hands stripped to their small-clothes and slowly, hesitantly trudged into the water.

There were a few moments of silence while the hands swam out. I said to Duco, "Captain, what do we get?"

He turned. "What do you mean?"

"Well, you have the Spanish ship and now Flint's silver because of us. What do the Doctor and the Squire and I get?"

Duco looked around at the shoreline of the lagoon and the green hills surrounding us. The clouds were low and grey and the light rain continued unabated. Like seals diving, the sailors' heads disappeared. "You get to live. You get.. one fifty-fifth share."

I nodded. Living was good. One fifty-fifth was not so good. A few moments later, one sailor splashed to the surface. Duco lumbered into the water, up to his waist, waiting for the delivery. He rinsed off the ingot, and walked slowly to shore, as big as Neptune, with a huge grin.

"We'll stack them here and move them to the ship later," Duco told one of the non-swimmers.

While Duco's attention was on the salvage operation, I took Sam Dresser aside and explained what I wanted.

"Excuse me, Captain," Sam said, and Duco turned to him. "How about a celebration tonight for the crew? The Doctor and Squire were cooks on the Hispaniola, they could cook up a stew for all hands up in the cave, could be ready by dark." Sam paused, just as I'd coached him. "Nice and dry in there."

Duco nodded. He said, "This is a good idea. You know, there are spirits aboard that Spaniard, and I think the crew wants to get drunk.. not in my ship, but in the cave, is fine." A moment later he said, "Can't miss stays in a cave."

Duco waved Trelawney and Livesey over. "We will have a feast tonight in that cave. You will make stew and roast a goat."

Knowing their parts in the play, Livesey said, "Aye, Captain, have the crew come to the cave at dusk." The Doctor and the Squire walked into the treeline, headed up to the cave, and I headed off to present some of my former shipmates with a proposition.

Just above the high tide mark, a pile of wet, dull-grey silver bars began to grow.

Schooner

Hispaniola

Chapter 17

The Celebration

A sailor is a miserable rat in the rain. Ben's cave, with two fires going, was dry and inviting. Some of Duco's men merrily rolled in some hogsheads of spirit, Spanish rum I believed, and set them up well inside. They had also brought a sack filled with bowls and mugs.

The smell of Livesey's stew made my mouth water, but it was not for us; he had roasted some goat-meat and set it aside.

Duco's men straggled in; one brought a little six-string instrument he called a 'guitarron', set up in a back corner, with a mug of rum, and began playing. Flanked by Ruen and Grimwood, Duco came in, ducking his head, and seated himself well back in the cave; I noticed he took no rum.

The drink loosened the pirates' tongues, and there was soon a babble of talk in various languages. A line formed for the Doctor's stew. Livesey had two wooden bowls set aside for Duco, who took them and returned to his place.

I sat near the guitarron-player, untouched mug of rum near me, and prayed Duco would not notice the absence of most of the Hispaniolas. Von Loendersloot was missing. Grimwood came and sat gingerly near me, having already got around two or three mugs of rum. I asked him where the Kapitein was.

"Why, he's aboard his new ship, then."

"I don't follow," I said.

"Duco's made the Kapitein second in command, in charge of the Spaniard, and don't you think Mr Ruen is ready to kill him?" Grimwood started his horrible sneering, leering laugh at this last, and Ruen indeed sat swilling rum and glowering at the cave wall, fingering the knife he always wore.

It was full night out, and raining hard. Livesey murmured to me that by his estimate only a few of Duco's crew were not at the party, that these were likely aboard the two ships. I whispered the news of the Kapitein, and he nodded and continued to ladle out stew to the pirates.

A group was dancing in a circle before the guitarron player; not proper dancing really, mere rhythmic contortions and stamping. Their elongated shadows writhed madly on the cave walls and ceiling. Things were proceeding nicely. Duco de Rijk finally had some rum and some stew, and was back in his place, tapping his toes to the music, eyes closed. Livesey took him more stew. A squabble broke out between two of Duco's Carib hands, but all he did was clap his hands sharply, and they subsided.

The music grew louder and the dancers more frenzied, fueled by regular trips to the rum barrels. One hand began bawling tunelessly and wordlessly along with the player's strumming, and was soon up stamping in the circle with the rest. Livesey continued to offer generous helpings of stew to all takers.

The party went on, getting stranger and stranger. An hour on, to my shock, Brighouse stumbled in from the rain, panting and plastered with mud, and fell in the dirt at Duco's feet.

He gasped, "Captain! There's a plot to kill you all and take both the ships!"

Duco stared at Brighouse in amazement. Livesey and I held our breaths.

Brighouse went on in a rush, "The Americans are out! They took the Black Swan! I broke loose! They're coming!"

Grimwood, very drunk indeed by this time, shouted, "Cap! He knows where all the berries are bodied!"

Duco began laughing, as if this was the funniest thing he'd ever heard. Wiping his eyes, he said, "Aye, the Americans are coming to kill us!" And he bent over again with laughter. The entire crew started laughing, braying, and Brighouse stared around in disbelief. He jumped to his feet and ran out of the cave. The party continued as if nothing had happened.

In a moment, Duco, shaking his head in confusion, followed Brighouse outside into the rain. Livesey nodded to me, and, taking a piece of hardwood with me as a weapon, I followed as quickly as I could. Behind me the light and sound of the pirate feast quickly faded.

Two paths led away from Ben's cave: one led south through the woods to Kidd's Anchorage and the Spanish ship; the other led down to the headwaters of the North Inlet where the Black Swan was anchored. I decided that Duco would head for his home, the Black Swan, and so I ran down that path in the dark. Within forty paces I tripped over something soft and fell headlong, losing my club. It proved to be Brighouse. There was no pulse. I resumed running for the silver cache on the beach. There weren't supposed to be any boats, but Duco could easily run along the beach on the northwest side and get close enough to swim to his ship.

When I reached the high-tide mark, there was no Duco and no boat. The stack of ingots was still there, waiting to be loaded. Not knowing what else to do, I climbed on the silver and sat, ears cocked, staring into the rain. There were no lights visible from the Black Swan, and the forested hillsides were completely black.

Fifteen or twenty minutes later, I heard a bellowing down the inlet, it sounded like the southwest shore. I could not make out the words through the rain, but it sounded like Duco. And he was getting closer. I could hear him screaming in Welsh, and then I knew Livesey had been right. For the goat stew he fed Duco's crew was chock-a-block with his 'Flesh of the Gods' mushrooms, reputed to cause visions and, we hoped, unconsciousness.

So a berserk Duco the Giant was coming toward me in the dark. I stood tensely next to the stack of ingots, debating whether to run for the treeline, or to confront the strongest man in the world, out of his head, with no weapon at all.

Duco's voice, ever louder, came echoing across the water, over the drumming of the rain on the sand.

"Mam! Mam, madda imi! Gwylltio fi ddaru'r dynion yna! Meirw 'nawr i gyd!" (Mother! Forgive me! Those men angered me - now they are dead!)

And I could see Duco's great form out of the gloom, coming directly toward me. He pointed at me. "Ti! Twyllwr! Ddim castia mwy!" (You! Trickster - no more tricks!)

Duco was stumbling right at me, hands outstretched. The only weapon at hand was an ingot of silver. With both arms, I raised it over my head, waited, and let fly. It hit Duco in the shoulder and he didn't even react. Desperately I snatched another ingot, and this time threw with my right arm only. It caught Duco the Giant directly in the forehead, and he crashed to the sand in front of me.

"Well played, medicoe, prime hurling!" Behind me several boats crunched onto the shore. It was Lt McCully, the Hispaniolas, and his marines and sailors, free. McCully stepped ashore and walked to Duco, who was face down in the sand. Several Americans, without instruction from McCully, hurried up the path to the cave, carrying some small kegs.

"Where have you all been?" I shouted at him.

"Searched the ship - needed some supplies. Rope him well," the Lieutenant said to the group of marines. They trussed Duco to several oars and hefted him to their shoulders. The rain stopped suddenly, and the marines carried Duco de Rijk up the path toward his crew and the cave.

A small crowd, including the Hispaniolas, remained on the beach. Allan slapped me on the back. We were all silent for a few moments.

Lt McCully asked, "How do things stand at the cave? Dresser told us the plan, after they broke us out of the hold."

I said, "They were pretty well out of their heads when I left, but that won't last forever." I looked at them and in the boats. I hoped for more guns. We'll have to guard the cave entrance pretty carefully, because they outnumber us three to one."

McCully said breezily, "Maybe not." He addressed the Hispaniolas clustered around. "You men did a good job breaking us out."

I burst out, "Why did you take all this time, with those madmen in the cave, and Duco looning about, killing folk with his bare hands? You could have ruined everything!"

McCully said cooly, "Dresser told me of your plan to incapacitate the pirates in the cave. I needed some additional supplies, and I also sent a crew to sail to the Spaniard and take her."

"'Sail'? Last night it was a hard two hour pull," I said.

McCully shrugged. "The wind shifted." He limped over to the stack of silver. "This is the famous silver cache, eh? How much is here in dollars?"

"I have no idea. The pirates could decide to leave the cave any time - and what was so bleeding important?"

Up the hill on my right bloomed a bright orange glow, followed by the roar of a black-powder explosion.

McCully grinned and said, "Fast-burning fuse."

Chapter 18

The Divvying

The next morning, on the beach, the Hispaniolas roasted a goat. It seemed Quixotic, but we were hungry, waiting tensely for the Americans, not knowing their intentions. I stood under the treeline in the grass, feeding handfuls to the grey mare, who was following me around like a faithful hound. A few men strayed to the pile of silver, touching or boldly hefting an ingot. Some of the crew bathed in the shallows, but emerged hastily as the remaining American sailors and marines came out of the woods. McCully raised his hand in greeting, and I was tempted to utter "Ugh!" or "How!" like a red Indian, but felt it might be somewhat out of place.

The two crews hunkered down in two semicircles around the fire, with Lt McCully, Cummings and Timmins the marine sergeant sitting with Livesey, the Kapitein, the Squire, and myself.

McCully spoke to me. "I'll get right to it, Hawkins, because I don't know these gentlemen, being owners and captain of a foundered vessel, and I don't know their

position. But I do know your crew will listen to you."
Von Loendersloot glowered but said nothing.

I said cautiously, "That may be. What do you have in
mind, Lieutenant?"

"Divvying. We have two ships here, Spaniard and slaver.
I consider myself and crew duty-bound as American
patriots to do the best we can for our nation. In theory,
that means taking the Black Swan and your treasure of
silver."

At this, Yellow Jack growled audibly and stood facing Lt.
McCully, pistol in one hand, naked cutlass in the other.

"However," McCully said, "you are as numerous and well-
armed as we." He stopped.

I said, "I find our natural roles to be allies, as we were
yesterday, not opponents - your unjust impressment of us
notwithstanding. The Doctor here tells us the Spaniard is
well-found in armaments and supplies, if not horses."
McCully smiled thinly at that. I said, "I would hope that
the Spaniard is an acceptable prize."

McCully stared at the sand intently for a moment. "Capt.
Conyngham charged me with taking that slaver -" he
jerked his thumb at the Black Swan, a mile down the inlet
- "and selling it as a prize."

By this time the goat was well roasted and we served out
with banana leaves for plate, and we all began eating.
Livesey leaned forward and addressed Lt McCully.
"Might I ask your estimate regarding the relative worth of
the two vessels?"

McCully scratched his head. "Well, now, I might say as a warship, the Spaniard would have the edge - but again, the slaver has all those cannon. But she isn't fitted as a frigate, most irregular. One problem with the Spaniard - all her charts have gone missing. They needed 'em to get here for the horses, all right, and we looked near the stern in case they were pitched overboard when that pirate took her. But no. Maybe Duco took them and hid them on his ship. I can't ask him, so I'm asking you - are the Spaniard's maps aboard the slaver?"

"No, Lieutenant, " I answered truthfully, "they are not."

"A pity. The maps are worth more to my nation than either ship."

Livesey stood. "Lieutenant, I am in possession of the Spaniard's maps. Do we have your agreement that once turned over to you, each of our crews will go our separate ways?"

I stood, and so did McCully. He said, "Aye, it's a deal." And we all shook hands.

Schooner

Hispaniola

Chapter 19

Aboard the Black Swan

So the Hispaniolas were reunited, though sadly reduced. English missing were Allard, Mersey, Dick, and Eben, plus the Dutch, who I did not know well, all drowned in the aft hold of the American Revenge. And of course Duco had done for Brighouse. The Hispaniolas, both English and Dutch, who had for a short while been pirates under Duco, responded to Kapitein von Loendersloot's orders with no alacrity whatsoever. However that changed when he detailed a boat's crew to bring the silver aboard. I never saw men move so fast.

The pirates and Duco had been left a shovel, and no doubt were busily digging themselves out as fast as ever they could. The Kapitein assigned Allan the job of keeping watch on the cave-mouth. If Duco broke free, Allan was to fire a gun and run for the beach and my old friend the jolly-boat.

There was much for this small crew to do to ready the Black Swan for a voyage. A three-mast frigate is so much more complicated a machine than a two mast schooner, that we could not simply weigh anchor and set to sea.

It was late morning before the silver was loaded and the water barrels topped up. The Kapitein, Doctor, Squire and myself were in Duco's oversize main cabin perusing charts when a deputation led by Sam Dresser requested our presence on deck. When we emerged, Von Loendersloot looked aloft, and asked Laemmers, who was standing next the quarterdeck stairs with a peculiar expression on his face, "First mate, why are the men not aloft preparing the rigging?"

"They will not, Mynheer Kapitein."

The crew, English and Dutch, were standing in a knot just abaft the mainmast. Sam Dresser, holding a piece of paper, was flanked my Yellow Jack and Dutch Jan. Sam called, "Cap'n, it's equal shares or it's no good with us."

"Bloody hell! This is mutiny and you will hang!" shouted the Kapitein.

"It don't have to be, Cap, if you and the Squire and Doctor, there, will just sign this here paper - " started Sam Dresser.

Yellow Jack broke in, "There's five, maybe six hundred thousand pound there, and we want some. That old fool -" and he pointed to the Squire, "- all of you lied to us, this weren't no tradin' voyage, this were always aboot that silver -- you put our lives in, in, -"

"Jeopardy," said Sam Dresser.   "Cap, we wants equal shares, or we don't sail.   Duco's going to break out soon, and all we have to do is wait for him.   So, mateys, just make it easier on us all and make your marks on this here agreement, and we'll all go shares and sail this pirate ship right back to England for you."

At that moment we heard the far off shot of a musket. Sam Dresser said, "That'll be Duco, and won't he be mad... Cap, what do you want to do?"

For some time I had been considering what I'd seen and heard, and had resolved to verify my suspicions.   I backed away from the group at the companion-way, found and lit a lanthorn, and went below.   It took only two minutes to check, and I re-emerged on deck, hoping none would notice my wet, befouled feet and legs.

Von Loendersloot's little pistol was on the deck between the two groups - someone must have struck it from his hand.   I came up behind Livesey and spoke in his ear for a few moments.   He looked at me sharply, and I nodded reassuringly.

I looked down toward the headwater of the inlet, and saw Allan pulling madly for the ship.   Livesey pointed, and all aboard saw Duco, a mile away, leading a very angry pirate crew running for the beach.

Sam Dresser turned back and said, "Pressure's on you, not us, gentlemen, we'll make more with Duco, unless you sign right here."   Jack had found a pen and inkwell somewhere aboard.

"You're right, Sam," said the Doctor.

The Kapitein almost howled, "But the Squire two hundred thousand pounds owes!" Looking malevolently at the Doctor, he said, "And you are owner of nothing, your ship will not sail again; you have no say here."

The Doctor nodded. "And thus you are Kapitein of nothing, and have no say here." Turning to the crew, he said, "That's the way of it, men, the Squire owes a pile of money to the men Kapitein von Loendersloot works for. And if we go equal shares, the Squire goes to debtors-prison. For good."

"Not my problem, mate," said Sam Dresser. "You lot lied to us, let us get pressed and drownded in the hold of that American, and then along comes Duco, throwing parties overboard to the sharks."

We heard the bump of the jolly-boat alongside, and soon Allan popped over the side. On the shore, Duco de Rijk and his murderers were panting along; Duco appeared to be attempting to load a musket as he ran.

Livesey said to Sam, "Here's what I propose. I'll sign your paper if I take ownership of the Black Swan." He looked around at the crew. "Unless you gentlemen intend to add piracy to mutiny and theft."

Sam Dresser's eyes narrowed. "We go equal shares on the silver, and you get the ship, is that right, sir?"

Livesey looked at me. I nodded. He said to Sam, "Yes, that's the agreement, I don't know how much this ship is worth, especially with the war on, but it should help the Squire somewhat."

Sam Dresser surveyed the running pirates, now about a quarter mile away, and he looked at the Hispaniolas, who all nodded or murmured their assent. "It's a deal." He looked up. "No flogging or riding the crew."

"Done," said Livesey.

Later, the Doctor, Squire, Kapitein and I all signed a paper stating crudely but legibly that each of the listed crew were to enjoy equal shares of the silver hoard acquired on this date at this latitude and longitude. All the Hispaniolas had previously made each his sign or mark, so the document was complete. And legal.

Behind me I heard Squire Trelawney sigh and say to himself, "First the maps, now the treasure. I am going to prison, certes."

In moments, without being issued any orders, the crew cut the anchor, went aloft, and the Black Swan turned obediently and headed to sea on the ebb. The pirates, noticeably fagged, continued to slog along the beach. Duco de Rijk had far outstripped his crew and reached the mouth of the North Inlet just as the Black Swan did. Duco, like those maroons so long ago, in this very place, fired a shot at the ship out of rage and frustration. It sang harmlessly overhead. He then snapped the musket, his only musket, across his knee.

Livesey was watching this performance. "Squire, you used to be a crack shot."

"Yes?"

Livesey pointed at Duco's shrinking figure. "That fellow is enterprising... and we have his ship."

"No, old friend," said Trelawney, "I can't shoot the fellow down in cold blood."

I said, "Besides, he's out of range already."

We were now on the open ocean, shouldering aside the sea, with the island on our port bow, only making two or three knots.

Allard, the sharp-eyed lookout, cried, "Look -- a horse! Port side!"

"It's your grey horse, Jim," said Trelawney. I squinted, and there in the water, already a hundred yards off the beach north of Foremast Hill, was a horse, swimming directly toward us. It did appear to be the grey. "She's coming after you, my boy," winked the Squire.

I turned to Yellow Jack and Sam Dresser, the Kapitein being so blown that none could consider him. "Heave to! I say, lads, I beg you, heave to! That's my horse in the water!"

Dresser grunted, "Your horse? No bleeding time for horsies, Hawkins."

I said, desperately, "She came here on a ship! She's swimming for us! ...for me."

Yellow Jack punched Sam lightly on the shoulder, which sent him reeling. "Where's your sense of, of..."

"Poetry and that rot," sighed Sam. He turned. "Heave to, you lot! Let's rig some blocks -- no jigger, too small, we'll need a luff --" But the rest was lost to me, because I dived headfirst off the rail of the Hispaniola.

The sea wasn't running too high, two or three-foot waves, and I dogpaddled toward the horse, which I could see about every tenth wave, still coming, swimming strongly. By the time we met, the Black Swan was half a mile away, turning in a curve designed to intersect ours, I prayed. The grey was breathing deeply, head high, and whinnied when I swam up to her. Of course, she'd come to the New World on a ship, she knows what that is, I thought. I swam by her side, hanging on to her long mane. After a moment I swung up on her back. It was then I noticed she had a rope around her neck - a rope that hadn't been there when I last fed her ashore.

As these thoughts passed by me, I was pulled off backwards by a grip on my shirt. The waves closed over my head and I thrashed and turned over in the water, trying to see my attacker, my eyes stinging from the salt water, and a fist with a long knife swept past my nose. I'd seen that knife.   I sculled madly backwards, trying to make some space, and rose to the surface for a long gasping breath.   A head broke the waves a few feet from me - Paleface Ruen.   He had been towed underwater by the Grey, perhaps urging her into the water in the first place. Ruen drew back his arm as if to throw his knife, but I dodged, and perhaps my head was too small a target, for he did not, but rather began swarming toward me. Meanwhile, the Grey had begun to circle us, rope trailing behind her, rather than swim for the ship. Ruen lunged again, and succeeded in tearing a huge rent in the front of my billowing shirt. That was too close. I took a huge breath and sank underwater - the water might slow him down.

This time my stinging eyes served me better, for I was able to see somewhat. I had dodged off to the side, away from that terrible knife, and saw that he, too, had dropped beneath the surface, looking for me. I was almost behind him. The rope trailing from the Grey dropped over his shoulder in a languid curve. Seeing a chance, I swam forward, seizing the rope, looped it over his head and neck, then brought both feet up into the middle of his back, pulling the rope tight around his neck, pushing with my feet and pulling with my arms. The Grey kept circling, turning us all around in the water. Ruen thrashed about a moment then began cutting at the rope just in front of him. I could not see what happened, but a bluish little cloud of blood appeared - he had cut his own hand or arm, quite badly. In a moment the rope parted and I let go. He began to turn in the water toward me.

The Grey was off to my left, and the shortened rope drifted past, and I grabbed on to it, kicking like mad for the surface, away from Paleface. The good horse chose this moment to resume her course for the ship. Lungs bursting, I surfaced and saw that the Black Swan was dead in the water about a hundred yards away. The Grey continued to head for the ship. To my horror, I saw the fin of a huge great white shark angling toward us. It passed us at full speed, and a moment later I heard a great strangled cry from Ruen, fifty feet or more behind us. I turned to see, and the shark had him, frantically stabbing at its head, in its jaws. One last scream from Ruen, and then he was pulled underwater.

The familiar side of the Black Swan glided up to us, and there was a rope-and-sail contraption swung from the mainsail crosstree. The sail was floating on the surface of the water. Several of the crew, having seen the shark, were hanging over the side with muskets, hoping to shoot anything approaching us. Sam leaned over the rail and shouted instructions to pull the sailcloth under her belly and hook it back up. I had to dive deep below to escape those thrashing hooves, and I swallowed a lot of seawater before it was fixed. "Tend your guys --" called Sam. "Haul away!" And up she went. I had to make do with a rope ladder over the side, banging my shins and scraping my hands on barnacles, but made it over the rail in time to see the entire crew ease the grey through an open hatch through the gundeck into the hold. Dripping, I ran below. She stood there like a veteran as I removed the harness. The entire crew cheered, I am not abashed to say. Though what I was to do with a horse I had not considered. Yet here she was, a pet.

Later, after the hubbub over the horse had died down and we got under weigh, Livesey grasped me firmly by the shoulder and followed by Trelawney, led me to Duco de Rijk's outsize cabin, which reminded me of Lemuel Gulliver's encounters with the Brobdnagians. Livesey almost hissed, "I had to give those valuable maps to McCully, and now we just signed away the silver on your say-so. I hope you have an explanation."

I nodded. "I know how you must feel. We had no choice. Duco would have got the silver and he would have fed us to the sharks in the bargain."

"And so if we get back, Jim," wheezed the Squire, "It's back to prison for me." He looked miserable.

"Trust me. I will have to show you both when we are unobserved," I replied. "It may take some time." I turned to look at the island, shrunk to a sliver in the late afternoon. "Three and a half days."

Livesey said, "What was that?"

"This time I was on the island only three and a half days."

The crew was in exuberant spirits, singing aloud at unaccountable moments, winning and losing fortunes while gambling until Yellow Jack, at the Doctor's suggestion, declared that winnings or no, upon landing in Bristol every person aboard would get his equal share of the silver hoard.

Two days later, with all hands aloft excepting me, I signalled Livesey and Trelawney to follow me below. They followed me down to the gun deck, down a hatch ladder to the hold, with a hello to the grey, and then to another hatch to the bilges. Trelawney held back. "These are my only clothes, Jim, to be worn all the way to England, if we live. I hesitate to besmirch them with no good reason."

I grinned. "There is a good reason, and you can always take a swim to clean off."

"Very well, then," he grumbled.

Lanthorn lit, we crouched in the smelly, Stygian gloom. I silently handed the lanthorn to Livesey, and extracted a clasp-knife. We were crouched next to a double row of regular stones of pig iron running along the ship's keel, serving as ballast. The stinking bilge-water splashed us as the ship pitched. This far below, the only sound was the sea beneath us and our own breath.

"Enough mystery, James, on with it," said the Doctor.

I wiped the top of one of the ballast stones clean, and scraped a line on it with my knife. The long scratch gleamed back at us like a bright future.

I looked Squire Trelawney in the eye and said, "I'd like to speak with you regarding your daughter Lilith."

Chapter 20

AFTERWORD

This narrative has finally caught up with itself, like Ouroborous the worm; that is to say, to the present day.

The alert reader will have ascertained that Captain Duco de Rijk, that thrifty, teetotaling, hardworking pirate businessman, had consolidated the gains of a dozen years' piracy into the least likely spot, the bilges of his own ship.

Once moored safely in Bristol, we shed the crew and its 'equal shares', and (with somewhat more difficulty) shed Kapitein von Loendersloot, who was convinced Trelawney was headed for debtors' prison. We then moved the Black Swan to a Bristol shipyard and, under armed guard, had its ballast removed to Livesey's bankers, who were quite overcome by the wealth loading into their strongroom by the barrowful. Duco's melted-down treasure proved to be many times the worth of Flint's paltry ingots.

But that was all nothing compared to our efforts to find Miss Trelawney and simultaneously to clear the Squire's debt; for indeed we were a week late in returning.

Miss Trelawney had had her own adventures; being a spirited woman, she determined not to stay where the bailiffs could easily scoop her up, and slipped out of her aunts' cottage at midnight and secretly made her way to the northern estate of a dear school-friend. Wollett pursued her doggedly across England and did at last arrive at the estate with a writ, and packed her off in a carriage for Wormwood Scrubs.

By this time Trelawney's creditors were mollified, and we had the best intelligence money could buy; I was waiting at the very gates of the prison, with both countermanding writ and the grey mare, saddled for Miss Trelawney.

I am happy to say we rode away from care down a tree-lined road on a perfect English summer day.

To my joy, Lilith Trelawney soon consented to be my wife, and we now have two children, a girl and boy, the apple of their grandfather's eye. Over time, I secured a comfortable Dorset estate within riding distance of Livesey, Trelawney, and my mother. Our extended family has been exceedingly happy and, needless to say, extremely prosperous. I was recently able to socially meet Mr. Bellingham And Unmarried Daughter of Oxford Town. It was a great pleasure to do so.

However, all is not well. In the past two weeks, Trelawney, Livesey and I have all received identical letters. In their entirety, each reads: "You Three have something of mine. I am coming to reclaim it. DdR."

Livesey and Trelawney, those old warriors, are adamant in their intent to not flee this threat of Duco's. They have, however, arranged for a waiting ship which can a moment's notice whisk them away upon an extended visit to Majorca, for which Livesey has long had a fond spot.

Lilith speaks fluent French, and is quite at home there. We are therefore all completely packed and ready to travel, and await the coach for the Brittany packet. Since our nations are now at peace, I am taking Lilith and the children to France, and anticipate a long and uneventful stay among her many friends there, aristocrats all.

J. Hawkins
Dorset, England
1785

FINIS

Author's Afterword

The Caribbean, 1778. Jim Hawkins, the Doctor, and the Squire are on their way back to Treasure Island to retrieve a fortune in silver. To get home safely, they must first evade the American Navy, the Spanish Navy, and the largest pirate captain in the world.

A few comments about Stevenson's 'Treasure Island'. Its original, discarded title was 'The Sea Cook'. A child, reading this as an adventure, will be taken by the straightforward plot and striking characters. An adult, (re)reading the same book, is struck by Long John Silver's dual nature -- on the surface, a genial, talkative old sailor, yet ready at a moment to murder. Three years later Stevenson wrote 'Strange Case of Dr. Jekyll and Mr. Hyde' (no 'The') which is another, more direct psychological examination of an artificially-created dual personality in one body, as well as a taut, well-paced horror-thriller. An adult, reading 'Treasure Island', will see the storm coming long before the narrator, young Jim Hawkins, does. In a sense, it's written in layers, one for the boy, one for the man.

Because of its fame as the pre-eminent pirate novel, one might imagine that 'Treasure Island' sprang full-grown from Stevenson's pen. There are in fact some recognizable precedents, well available to Stevenson. Edgar Allan Poe used a young man as both a main character and as first-person narrator in a sea-novel featuring mutiny, piracy, and cannibalism, along with adventures on shore, in his only full-length novel, 'The Narrative of Arthur Gordon Pym of Nantucket', 1838. Always the horror writer, Poe includes a ship of corpses, and a dead man with a red cap, revived by Stevenson as O'Brien, killed by Israel Hands in

'Treasure Island'. Some historians also claim that the comic, tragic, cheese-fixated character Ben Gunn is a caricature of Daniel Defoe's protagonist in 'Robinson Crusoe'.

One of the reasons that 'Treasure Island', published in 1883, became so widely read, indeed, one of the most popular works of the late nineteenth and twentieth centuries, was the spotty enforcement of international copyright law. Less than two decades earlier, in order to pay his bills, Charles Dickens was forced a second time to go on tour in America, reading from his works, because copyright law was in its infancy, and no international enforcement agency then existed. With no royalties due Stevenson's estate, it was an attractive, inexpensive proposition, and there were myriad unauthorized versions of the book published in English-speaking countries, and probably beyond. The 1911 'Wyeth' edition, featuring artwork by N.C. Wyeth, is justifiably the most famous of them all.

*****

Loving 'Treasure Island' as I do, and still possessing the 1927 illustrated edition (Saalfield Publishing, Ohio, copyright-free) I enjoyed so as a boy, some years ago my mind started cogitating about What Happened After The End. How would young Jim Hawkins utilize his share of Flint's treasure, once home in England? What could a commoner, a taverner's son, suddenly possessing wealth, do with it?

Naturally I considered Jim might emulate the ever-sensible and intelligent Doctor Livesey. Oxford medical school, required no pedigree, only money. How would Livesey handle his infusion of money? Wisely. The

Squire Trelawney was the one who hired Silver and his gang of cutthroats, on the basis of them being 'old salts'... a fool, in other words. So the Squire might easily overextend himself financially, with debtor's prison as the prod to action.

Stevenson left the motivation for a sequel in the bar silver our heroes had left behind on the island. Add the Squire's possible financial woes -- debtor's prison -- to the lure of several hundred thousand pounds in still-buried silver, and there is the motivation for a 'Return To Treasure Island'. But why should Jim, on his way to a comfortable living as a surgeon, risk his life -- again? Enter the Squire Trelawney's hitherto-unmentioned beautiful daughter Lilith, also in danger of imprisonment. Add a time limit, the ticking clock, for urgency.

However, at first I simply had the setup. There was no antagonist, as I decided that intense media overload -- Robert Newton's 'aar, matey' Silver from the 1950 Disney film, animated movies, chain restaurants -- had moved the Long John Silver character far from Stevenson's conception right into caricature. Thus I had the challenge of writing a compelling story minus the most famous character. There was no second or third act. My sole idea was that our heroes should return victorious and rich(er). I stalled, came to a complete and utter stop, as soon as they stepped on board the old Hispaniola -- because as a desert-dweller, I knew little about the age of sail or shiphandling.

A friend of mine, percussionist extraordinaire Will Hillis, told me, "You need to read some Patrick O'Brian." O'Brian wrote a series set in the Napoleonic era, following a Royal Navy captain and his friend, a surgeon. Some may recall Peter Weir cribbed plot elements from at least four of O'Brian's books and created the film 'Master and Commander' with Russell Crowe as the lead and Paul Bettany hopelessly miscast as his sidekick.

I began reading the O'Brian series out of duty and research and soon fell in love. There are twenty volumes in this series, and I read the entire thing through three to five times. Call it fifteen million words or so. I also spent many hours rereading Jane Austen. So the period language came naturally, and anyone can research anything using the Internet. But meanwhile, my characters were frozen, waiting on or about Page 68, on the refitted schooner Hispaniola, moored at the Bristol docks.

Toward the end of this several-years-long reading binge, I had so much Age of Sail information in my head that my antagonist, the entire second act, and the third act, came to me unbidden, in the shower, just as you hear about. I outlined like crazy before it faded, writing out some of the scenes/chapters that seemed most vivid (the movies call 'em 'tentpole' scenes), and finished the first draft in longhand while in India some years ago.

Possibly because I had eliminated Long John as a character, one of my desires was to otherwise follow Stevenson's structure as much as possible. First was using Jim Hawkins' first-person narration as the primary observer and voice. Next was to 'cut away' to Doctor Livesey for a period when our main characters were separated. The narration then continues, by Jim, through to the end of the book. There are even twenty chapters, like Stevenson's manuscript.

A complicating factor, besides the decision to avoid Long John Silver, was that I determined to use actual world events -- the American Revolution, Britain's war with France and Spain -- as a backdrop. Captain Gustavus Conyngham, a privateer attached to the 'infant' American Navy, did exist, and his ship was indeed called the Revenge. Setting the story in 1778, when much of the western world was at war, gave plenty of opportunity to place my heroes in peril.

I also wished to avoid as many pirate novel clichés as possible. A complete sea-battle was described from the point of view of the Hispaniola's crew imprisoned in the hold of an American Navy ship. Duco's pirate ship was a disguised, heavily modified slaver. It was identified as such by an American lieutenant with a sensitive nose -- it was exposed as a pirate, not a slaver, because it did not stink. The Americans determined to hang the giant pirate captain Duco while he was unconscious, only to have him revive and apparently dive into the Atlantic. The pirates, once in control, systematically tossed captured sailors, the ones unwilling to join, to the sharks. It could be said that the finale on the island, where the pirates were overcome by eating a stew made of mushrooms called 'Flesh Of The Gods', well known to botanists of the day, is moderately innovative, and reveals I am indeed a child of the Sixties. At any rate I had great fun challenging the reader's assumptions about twists and turns in a pirate novel.

Regarding sailing arcana, I sat with my National Geographic map of the Caribbean, a ruler, compass, and protractor, looking at prevailing winds and currents, calculating directions, distances and sailing times. Of course that wasn't enough. Fortunately we have a sailor friend, Kathy Hill, who used to organize the Chesapeake Bay Schooner Race, and may again, and I emailed entire passages to her, explaining what I wanted to happen. Thank you Kathy! By the time I was done, with her help, my written sailhandling and navigation shouldn't cause a real sailor to chortle. Or even snicker.

Writers claim writing is a solitary, agonizing process, where you squeeze blood out of your forehead before words land on the page. Nah. For me, that rich period of creating characters and circumstances, allowing them free rein, is one of the finest and highest mental states I have ever experienced. I want it back. That doesn't mean the next books have just flowed. I was fortunate, being a complete A.D.D. case, to have kept at this one long enough to finish it. Note the twelve year gap between finishing the first draft and actually publishing the work.

You may have noted there is room for a sequel to this sequel, in which Duco pursues Jim, Lilith, the Doctor and Squire across revolutionary-era France. Who knows if that particular ship will ever be launched. After all, being a desert dweller, all I know about France in that era is 'A Tale of Two Cities.' Next to nothing, in other words. All the same, miracles do happen.

As Jim Hawkins says in the beginning, "Human nature, acted upon by Providence, is at the heart of all good tales." My earnest hope is that this one did not disappoint.

Karl Moeller,
Tucson, Arizona,
February 2015

STUDY QUESTIONS

1. What kind of writer creates 'study questions' for his readers? Does he imagine that book clubs or English classes are going to hang on every word?
2. Does the book stand on its own if you have not read Stevenson's 'Treasure Island'?
3. If you have read the original 'Treasure Island', did the various characters' actions - Jim, the Doctor, and the Squire - match your previous impressions?
4. Did you miss the Long John Silver character? Why do you think the Silver character was left out of this storyline?
5. Did you find the giant pirate captain Duco to be a fully-formed character? Was the idea of an intelligent, businesslike giant pirate jarring? If so, why?
6. Did you recognize the jokes as they went past? Hints: 'Time & tide wait for no man', 'Cardiff Giant', and 'toredo (aquatic worm) = Toledo'.
7. Was the method used to subdue Duco's crew on the island a cheat?
8. Were you surprised by Jim's discovery in Duco's ship? Was that telegraphed in advance?
9. Lilith Trelawney's adventures eluding Wollett and the bailiffs was mentioned very briefly in the Epilog. Should her various adventures on the run in Britain have been interspersed with Jim and the Doctor's narratives?
10. What lay just ahead in France, in the final passage of the book, with Jim and his family ready to flee to France in 1785? Would France have been a safe haven? Does that sound like another sequel, Duco chasing them across Revolutionary France?

www.ingramcontent.com/pod-product-compliance
Lightning Source LLC
Chambersburg PA
CBHW070017120726
47909CB00003B/975